ZINNIA SPECIAL EDITION

BOOK THREE OF THE ANGELBOUND OFFSPRING SERIES

CHRISTINA BAUER

COPYRIGHT

Monster House Books
Brighton, MA 02135
ISBN 9781945723896
Second Edition

CONTENTS

EPILOGUE

ALSO BY CHRISTINA BAUER

APPENDIX

DEDICATION

**For All Those Who Kick Ass, Take Names
And Read Books**

COLLECTED WORKS

Angelbound Offspring

The next generation takes on Heaven, Hell, and everything in between

1. Maxon
2. Portia
3. Zinnia
4. Rhodes
5. Kaps
6. Mack
7. Huntress

Angelbound Origins

About a quasi (part demon and part human) girl who loves kicking butt in Purgatory's Arena

1. Angelbound
2. Scala
3. Acca
4. Thrax
5. The Dark Lands
6. The Brutal Time

4. ECHO Academy

This is a completed series.

Beholder

Where a medieval farm girl discovers necromancy and true love

1. Cursed
2. Concealed
3. Cherished
4. Crowned
5. Cradled

This is a completed series.

YEARS AGO

ZINNIA, AGE NINE

Tucking my unicorn comforter under my chin, I come to a big decision.

Nap time is for losers.

I may only be nine—well, almost ten—but I know one thing: there are way too many rules for dragon princesses like me. For starters, we're supposed to take naps every bleeding afternoon. No way. Napping is for babies. That's why I'm sneaking out today to see my best friend, LT.

Twisting under my covers, I check out my bedroom. There are pink curtains, white furniture, and the royal crest of Furonium over the door. My parents rule all the dragon shifters, so that crest-thingy hangs everywhere. My sisters, Kaps and Huntress, lie in their bunk beds across from mine. So you know, my family stays in human form most of the time. No dragon caves for us, thank you very much. Those places have bats.

Squinting, I look at my sisters more closely. *Are they really out of it? Can I sneak away?* Like always, Kaps lays half-off the top bunk. Wisps of brown hair hang over her mouth, blowing in and out with her snores. I shake my head.

Even asleep, my twin is noisy.

Meanwhile, Huntress rests curled up on her side. Her shoulders rise and fall silently. Huntress never lets out a sound, even when she's snoozing.

That settles it.

Both my sisters are totally zonked.

Time to go.

Walking on tippy-toe, I creep over to my dresser. My red party dress is already laid out on top. I brush my fingers across it. *So soft.* I slip on the fluffy prettiness, then choose matching patent leather shoes. Turning, I look at myself in the mirror: short white-blonde hair, pale skin, big blue eyes and—like most dragon shifters in Furonium—a long tail with an arrowhead-shaped end. Everyone says I look like Mum, while Kaps is a mini-Da.

But what does LT look like?

It's been months since my friend left for school. What if I don't recognize LT any more? Squishing my eyes shut extra-hard, I try to picture his face. Dark hair? Yes. Green eyes for sure. But mostly what I remember about LT is his music. *Acoustic guitar.* He plays tunes while I sing along; it's what we call *our beat.* Those songs echo in my mind …

All of a sudden my chest feels tight, like there's a rope around my ribs. I hate that LT left for music school. Don't get me wrong. I understand why my friend went to Earth to learn guitar stuff. Acoustic isn't exactly big with dragons. Plus LT's mum, Sienna, is both human and a famous cello player. So she knew the perfect school for LT.

That rope-feeling gets even tighter.

Shaking my head, I force on a smile. There's no reason to feel sad about LT today. He's back from school. Plus, my friend loves playing guitar in the afternoon. No doubt about it. Right now, LT sits on the bench under his favorite tree, plucking out a tune. Now it's up to me to leave the palace, cross the grounds to LT's cottage, and see him. My stomach twists like that time I ate kumba leaves on a dare from Kaps. *Must be getting excited.* Staying super quiet, I step across the wood floor and grab the door handle.

Almost there.

Sheets rustle nearby. Flipping her covers away, Kaps hops off the top bunk to land perfectly on the floor. She's wearing explorer khakis, the kind that are packed with hidden pockets. Her tail sways happily behind her. Both Kaps and I are Firelord tribe, so all our scales are black.

Crud. I made too much noise getting ready.

"Off for the royal treasury?" asks Kaps. My twin is obsessed with the miles of vaults under our palace. It's the dragon in her. With Kaps, everything is treasure, treasure, and more treasure. I could be wearing a bathing suit and she'd ask if I'm off to the royal vaults.

"Not really," I say slowly.

A figure appears out of thin air beside Kaps—someone with brown hair, violet eyes, and a white-scaled tail. It's Huntress. I didn't hear my older sister slip out of bed or anything, but that's Huntress for you. Glass dragons turn invisible and sneak around. It's what they do. Like always, Huntress wears battle leathers.

"You're off to see LT," states Huntress. When I was little, I used to wonder how Huntress always knew everything. Now I'm big and I have it all figured out. It's just Huntress being Huntress.

"LT?" asks Kaps. "Who's that?"

"Please." Huntress waves her hand. "We all know LT. He's been Zin's best friend since forever."

"But I'm Zin's twin," snaps Kaps. "That makes *me* her best friend." She glares in my direction. "There's no way you're off to see some dragon boy, right?"

I debate about lying, but it's pointless with my sisters. "Huntress is right. I plan on seeing LT today. Alone."

Huntress pins me with her mum-look. It's the one she uses when I'm about to burn my hand or make one of the servants cry.

"LT lives in a cottage to the west of the palace. You can't go there by yourself. That's dangerous."

I kick at the floor. *Another lecture about safety from Huntress.* Sometimes it's like my sister is a grown-up trapped in a ten-year-old's body.

"Come on," sighs Kaps. "There's no danger." My twin points at Huntress. "You give me the exact same speech every time I hit the vaults. Nothing ever happens. We're perfectly safe."

Following my twin, I point at Huntress, too. "See?" I ask. "Even Kaps agrees. The bad dragons are gone."

Huntress sets her hands on her hips. "Sure, the dragons of the Triumvirate stopped trying to break into the palace. But that was only five weeks ago. Mark my words. The Triumvirate hasn't given up. You don't know them like I do."

And Huntress is right.

The Triumvirate are renegade dragons loyal to the old emperor, Chimera. Not sure why they care—grandpa Chimera's been dead for years and was a total creep—but dragons can be weird. Now the Triumvirate hates my family and any tribe that follows us (which means they hate most everybody). In fact, it was the Triumvirate who destroyed Huntress' village. Back then, my big sister was a little kid and the only survivor. Afterward we adopted Huntress because—as Mum and Da said—anyone that strong was already a royal.

"I've got it." Kaps raises her hand. "Rumors are, someone found a map to Pandora's box. That thing has more than enough magic to stop the Triumvirate forever."

Kaps tells me all about odd treasures. Pandora's box is one of her favorites. Humans think Pandora was one of them, but she was really a dragon shifter and mage. Also, Pandora's magic comes from the arc of red stars that shine day and night over Furonium. We call them Pandora's starfall.

"Let me guess," I say. "Pandora's box might be hidden in the royal vaults."

"Yeah!" Kaps pumps her fist in the air. "Who's up for it?"

I creep closer to the door. "Looking around will take lots of time. You guys hit the treasury without me."

"No," says Huntress in her mum-voice again. "It isn't safe. The Triumvirate want revenge. Uncle Maxon killed Chimera. Now someone in our family must die and *make things even*." Huntress makes little quotation marks with her fingers when she says that last part.

"But we have plenty of family to go after," I say. "There's Grandma Myla, Grandpa Lincoln, Uncle Maxon—"

"Who are all super-strong warriors and wield amazing powers," interrupts Huntress. "The three of us?" She gestures between herself, me and Kaps. "We're the easiest targets."

It's all true, but it sucks. I twist at the skirt of my party dress. "I just want to hear LT play."

Huntress folds her arms over her chest. "That's why we'll *all* visit LT."

I don't like the way Huntress says the word *all*. "What do you mean?"

"Mum and Da will be there too," answers Huntress. "I figured you'd sneak off to see LT today, so I invited them along." Huntress' mouth arches into a sneaky half-smile. "Everyone wants to hear you sing."

A chill spreads over my body. "But I only sing for LT."

Kaps rolls her eyes again. "How hard can it be? *La la la.* Just sing."

"It's…" I begin to explain, but I can't find the words. For me, singing activates my magic. And I can't control that power yet. If I try to sing with other people round, magic just clogs up my throat. All I can do is hum. Unless it's only me and LT; then I can sing just fine.

"I don't get it," says Kaps. "Why do you only hum for us?"

"That's none of your beeswax," I reply. When we were little, I made the mistake of telling Kaps I thought LT was my rhana.

That's a dragon word for your life mate. Afterward, Kaps teased me for months. I still can hear her chants in my head.

Zin and LT sitting in a tree ... K-I-S-S-I-N-G!

If I told Kaps about how LT helps both my singing *and* my magic, then she'd never shut up.

Huntress ignores the whole LT situation. Instead, she moves to block the door. "We're all going with you. Or you can stay in bed, Zinnia. It *is* naptime, after all. I'll just alert the guards."

My mouth falls open in shock. "Not fair. Grown-up princesses shouldn't have to take naps." I look to Kaps. She has to agree with me on this one.

Kaps stands beside my older sister. "I'm with Huntress," she declares. "Nap now or show us what's *really* going on with LT and your singing."

I scrunch up my mouth and think things through. It's true that I can be sneaky like Kaps. And I'm also as good a warrior as Huntress. Still, I can't fight both my sisters at once.

"Fine," I say. "We'll *all* visit LT."

And so the three of us head out. But I take off at a run.

ZINNIA

I rush down a golden hallway. Four Kathikon stand nearby—they're our royal guard. Now if I were sneaking out alone, I could slip past the Kathikon easy. But with my sisters tagging along, I can't use my *very secret and super sneaky* ways out of the palace. So I speed right past the guards instead.

As I skitter along, one guard steps forward. She wears the usual Kathikon uniform: a long black suit with a bowler hat and cane. "Where are you off to, luv?" she asks.

While I keep running, I call to her over my shoulder. "Huntress is coming with me!"

Sure enough, my older sister starts down the hall behind me. Kaps strolls along at her side. Everyone knows Huntress can't tell a lie. That's why the Kathikon won't bother me or Kaps with questions—it's easier to ask Huntress.

My patent leather shoes are a little slippery, but I still make the turn to the next hallway at top speed.

Slam!

I run right into a bulky guy who's bursting out of his gray suit. *Master Killian.* Like everyone from the Thorntail tribe,

Killian has a charcoal-colored tail that ends in a spikey club shape. Since he runs his tribe, Killian also wears a red sash that reaches from his shoulder to his hip. Plus, his face is all over-sized: I'm talking a huge forehead, bulging cheeks and a mile-long chin. His little button eyes that match the ones on my plushie stuffed shark.

"Greetings, Princess Xi Iota Nu Alpha." Did I mention Killian's hair is slicked back with some kind of goop? He always leaves marks on our satiny high-back chairs.

"Hi, Master Killian."

"Fine day out, eh?" He's got a deep and gravelly voice that's all icky, like he just chugged milk. *Gooky voice.*

I walk sideways toward the exit. "Sure."

Most of the time, I talk to adults at least for a minute or two. Da says it's part of my job as princess. But I never chit-chat with Killian. His father, Oswine, helped out the evil Triumvirate. Then Oswine got caught, so he went to the dungeons for a while. Now Killian leads things and Oswine is out of jail. According to Killian, Oswine is now a good guy. Not sure I believe it.

Killian gives me a smile that doesn't reach his eyes. "Where are you off to?"

I take another half-step away. "Places." That not-a-smile from Killian always gives me the creeps.

Huntress and Kaps now round the corner. *Good!* I hate being alone with Killian. The Master Dragon's stuffie-shark eyes slowly scan all three of us. "The little princesses are on the move. Where are you bound?"

Kaps pats her adventure vest. "To find Pandora's box in the royal vaults."

Killian lifts his eyebrows. The guy doesn't show a lot of emotion, so this is a big move for him. "Are you now?"

Kaps loves nothing more than an audience for her treasure-talk. "Oh yes," she begins. "Don't you know the stories about Pandora's box?"

That creepy smile of Killian's actually reaches his eyes this time. "Tell me."

"Pandora's box is aligned with her starfall." Kaps spreads her arms wide toward an imaginary sky. My twin a really good story teller. "With it, you can bring back the power of any dead dragon."

Huntress, who'd been quiet so far, finally pipes up. "Bring back, *how?*"

Kaps slowly scans the hallway, like she's about to reveal a great secret. *Drama girl.* "Pandora's box puts dead powers into a live Furor. It's like you mush the ghost's abilities into a living dragon—" Kaps mashes her palms together to show the idea "—and then make a super-dragon. Of course, you can't pick a poopy dragon ghost. You should bring back someone with cool magic and stuff."

"And?" asks Huntress.

"And what?" counters Kaps.

"There are always conditions with these treasures of yours," says Huntress.

"Fine." Kaps throws up her hands. "You also need to put the ghost into someone of the same bloodline. And also-also, no one really knows the spells to make the whole thing work. But maybe there are instructions inside the box or something. Happy?"

"No, it sounds like far too much work," says Huntress.

"Shows how much *you* know." Kaps rolls her eyes.

All this time, Killian keeps up that sneaky-strange smile. *What's he up to?* I frown, wondering what to do about this guy. It's not like my parents don't know Killian is sketchy

That's when the Kathikon round the corner to check on us. My stomach turns all fluttery. *This is my chance.* With the royal guard nearby, my sisters are safe, even if Killian does smell funny and act weird. And since Killian is asking about treasure, Kaps and Huntress will be here for ages. That means one thing.

If I take off now, I should have just enough time to sing at least one song with LT.

Grinning, I race away at double-speed.

RHODES, AGE ELEVEN

I sit outside my family's cottage in Furonium. A great tree arches above me. Tiny yellow leaves twist and dive toward the ground. I'm aware of these things, but not as well. My real focus stays locked on my guitar as my hands seem to fly over the strings on their own. Images flood my mind.

I picture sunlight on water.

A baby laughing.

And Pandora's starfall glowing in the afternoon sky. Every year that starfall burns a little more brightly. After a millennium passes, the starfall will fade again. Bright and dim. Baby laughter and falling leaves. It all ties into the music, somehow.

That's when something activates my warrior's sense.

Cold.

Foul.

Danger.

Before, my surroundings were dim and dreamy. Now, everything snaps into sharp focus, from every wooden plank in my cottage home… to each cobblestone in the courtyard before me… and even to the line of trees that encircle them both.

A stranger is near.

Sienna steps into the front door. Some mothers are Mom. Mine's Sienna. Today she wears in a loose sheath dress of bright colors. It contrasts her cocoa skin and amber eyes. "That was a lovely tune. One of your own?"

"Yes. I wrote it with Zin."

"Why did you stop playing?" Sienna tilts her head. It isn't easy to hide things from her. "Is everything all right, Little Titan?" That's her nickname for me. Comes from my father's name, Titan.

I get my musician's skill from Sienna. But sensing danger? That's all Titan. Admitting to my warrior-side only makes Sienna lecture me on how fighting will confuse my art. And she's right. That said, I'm in no mood for one of her speeches now.

"I need a break," I reply. "My fingers are sore." *And this is true, although not the full story.*

"Don't play until they bleed, LT."

"I'll be careful."

Mom nods, shrugs and steps back inside. That's when Father steps up beside me. A towering figure, Father is seven feet of green skin and muscle who has a flattened nose, wide mouth, and the ability to wield lighting with ease.

A perfect Titan. He was named well.

Both Father and I scan the nearby tree line. Shadows darken there. New scents waft in from that spot. *Moth balls and sour milk.* Only one dragon creates that particular stench.

Sure enough, Oswine steps out from the line of trees. He's a bent figure with white hair and a smarmy grin. Sadly, he's also the ex-leader of the Thorntail tribe and a Triumvirate sympathizer. Father and I agree. Oswine should never have been released from the dungeons.

"Good afternoon, oh Enforcer of the Dragon Realms," calls Oswine. That's Father's official title. It means he keeps the royal family safe. Sure, our rulers have the Kathikon, but sometimes

you need a super-talented killer for special assignments. That's
where an Enforcer comes in.

My father lifts his chin. "Oswine. You're looking better."

So you know, *you're looking better* is a subtle jab at Oswine's
recent dungeon-stay.

"Yes, sunlight agrees with me." Oswine glances my way but
doesn't say hello. I'm half-human, so Oswine won't acknowledge
me unless he's forced into it. Such a lowlife.

"What do you want?" asks Father.

"A friendly chat," says Oswine. "I'm wondering if you know
anything about Pandora's box. Rumor is, it's on the wind."

The way Oswine spoke the words, *on the wind*? That's bad
news. A webwork of lightning churns inside my soul: warrior
magic. Titan and I are Electrophus dragons. We breathe lightning
instead of fire.

"I know the box been recovered," says Father slowly.

"Such a shame it turned up," Oswine sighs. "After all, no one is
sure what Pandora's box can do. That must worry you so. How
do you secure the royal family without a way to counteract this
unknown magic?"

"I'm not worried," says Father tightly.

Sadly, I know what it means when that particular twang
sounds in Father's voice.

He's worried.

"Ah, good." Oswine grins. "Then there's nothing to fret about."
Turning, he backs off into the forest again.

Breathing in deeply, I follow the scent trail. Once I'm certain
Oswine is well and gone, I focus on my father. "He's got Pandora's box."

"Perhaps." Father tilts his head. "Or he's trying to get it. I've
been tracking Oswine ever since he left the dungeons. He hasn't
done anything suspicious. Same with Killian." Father rubs his
neck in a nervous rhythm. "Pandora's box. That's trouble."

I shake my head. "Why? I thought Pandora's box only brought back a ghost, and then no one really knows how it works."

"I've heard the box builds up a charge, like how humans put power into batteries. Under certain conditions, you can use that stored magic to bring back a particular spirit. But it does other things as well."

Alarm rattles through my system. *This is huge.* "Such as?"

"That's the problem."

"Maybe should we put the royals in the tower. It's the most secure spot in Furonium." It's also not a real prison. More like a resort in a tall shape.

"No," states Father. "We still don't know for certain what, if anything, we're up against. Based on what Pandora's box can *really* do, the tower might be the worst spot for their safety. We simply need to stay vigilant." Father gestures toward my guitar. "That's a nice tune you were playing before. Haven't heard it in ages."

I eye Father. Should I push for more about the threat from Pandora's box? *Probably not.* If Titan is changing the subject, it means the topic's closed. And he's correct, too. The best we can do is stay alert and wait. It takes an effort, but I force my thoughts back to the tune I'd been playing.

"Yes," I reply. "It's one I wrote with Zin years ago." I don't say this part out loud, but I often play this tune. It's called *Our Song.*

"It's a fine tune." Father sets his hand on my shoulder. "And we'll figure this out, my son." Without another word, he steps back into the house.

I sigh. Pandora's box is loose. We don't know what it can do, so there's no way to protect against it.

My warrior's sense rails within me, urging me to do something. Anything. Yet there's only one action that remains.

Wait.

RHODES

*a*fter Father leaves, a long stretch of silence follows. The courtyard before our home turns empty and hollow. That's when I catch it: a new scent wafts on the air. *Peach blossoms and sunshine.* My heart beats at double speed.

Zin is coming.

She appears from the line of trees—a sprite of a girl in a red dress. Her white-blonde hair lays in a straight pixie cut that contrasts her round cherub face. Zin barrels into me, giving me a big hug. She moves so fast, I almost don't move my guitar aside in time. I hold her for a long moment, and it's like a part of my soul has returned.

Zin steps back. Her face is alive with excitement. I've seen this particular look before. Before she even speaks, I know what she'll say.

"I got the words to *Our Song!*"

I grin. This is the very tune I'd been playing before. I can come up with music, but I need Zin for lyrics. This one's been stuck for years—all we have is the title. Swinging my guitar back around, I start strumming once more.

Zin pulls a little book out of her pocket. It's something about classical music, but Zin's written all over some of the preprinted pages. She stares at the volume for a moment before scanning the clearing. "It's just us for now. I ran the whole way." She lowers her voice. "Other people are coming and, well, *you know*."

"Our beat."

Zin nods. "Our beat."

That's what we call the magic that rises in both of us when we play music together. *Our beat.* Zin doesn't talk about it because Kaps would tease her forever. I don't say anything since it's special, just for us. The rest of the world knowing would only expose something that doesn't belong to them anyway.

"I wish I could be like you," sighs Zin.

"What do you mean?" I ask.

"You can can still play guitar without me around."

"Sure, but it's different. I only sense my magic when you're near."

Zin's eyes get wide. "Even on Earth?"

I nod. "Sure, the teachers show me technique and stuff. But the magic isn't there unless you're nearby." I lean in closer. "You know why that is, don't you?"

"Because my magic is stronger." Zin hugs her elbows. She doesn't buy my theory about the magnitude of her powers. *And I get it.* How can you believe your magic is strong when you can't control it?

"How about this?" I ask gently. "I play and if you don't want to sing, don't."

Zin takes in a deep breath. "Okay."

I begin to play *Our Song*. The familiar tune fills the courtyard, lilting and sweet. After a few minutes, Zin starts to hum in time.

Tendrils of magic wind between us. Every note I pluck from my guitar gains a deeper ring. The very air hums with excitement and power.

Memories appear.

I picture the very first time I played this tune on my guitar.

Zin and I were talking about Chimera. Dragons have different colored scales which separate us into tribes. Furor with a human bloodline get extra colors on their tails. Chimera wanted to wipe out anyone who wasn't pure. In the end, the old emperor killed thousands of part-human Furor. But Zin's family sees things differently. Everyone is welcome now. We wanted a song that put their hope into music.

At last, Zin begins to sing.

Gray or green or brown or yellow
Your look could change just like the rainbow
I wouldn't care
It's what we share
You're mine

She pauses. "What do you think so far?"

"It's perfect," I say. "After all these years, you nailed it."

Zin bounces on the balls of her feet. "I have more words for the next verse." She flips through the pages of her little book and stops. I pause as well. No question why, either.

We're no longer alone in the courtyard.

All of a sudden, I notice our audience. There's Huntress and Kaps. The princesses are wide-eyed and silent. That rarely happens. My parents wait in the cottage doorway. Father's has wrapped his arm around Sienna's shoulder. And beyond them all stands the emperor and empress. I've only seen Zin's parents a handful of times, and then from across large spaces. Up close, Tempest looks all things broad, tall, dark and majestic. Portia is like Zin—spritely and pale—but with an unmistakable undercurrent of power.

I hop up to stand. "Your Majesties."

"I knew you two knocked about," says the emperor. "But this music?" He shakes his head. "It's beautiful."

"My sweet flower..." The empress beams at Zin.

"...Is growing bigger every day," finishes Zin. It's something they say often.

"Your magic is tied into music," adds the empress. "How lovely."

Zin stares at the cobblestone ground. "I didn't want to say anything until I could control it. That's why I only hummed before."

The empress looks to me. "And your friend helps you master your skills. Thank you, Rhodes."

Rhodes is my dragon name. It's short for Rho Delta Sigma. I didn't realize the empress knew it.

"Don't stop," adds the emperor.

I fidget from foot to foot. It's one thing to play for me and Zin. It's another to perform for the Emperor and Empress of all Furor.

"Please," adds the empress. Her eyes glisten with tears and that's when it hits me. *Our Song* touched them somehow. I scan the faces all around. Everyone seems a little misty. Even Kaps nods, and I'm pretty sure she hates my guts. I shoot another look at Zin. "You still have those words handy?"

"I do," she says.

I sit back down, reset my guitar, and resume playing. After a few seconds, Zin starts to sing once more.

Hold my hand and play in sunlight
The trees all flower with buds on branches
We laugh and play
We waste the days
There's time

Zin pauses. "That's all I have so far." She resets the little book into her pocket. "I'll finish the rest soon."

"Wow," I say. "It's coming along great." My heart does that

fast-pulse thing again. It's the magic we share. *Our beat.* "I missed you, Zin."

The moment I speak those words, I realize how little they say. *I missed you.* There's so much more that's happened. Being on Earth proved to me that Zin is more than a cherub-sweet face or talented musician. It's like with *Our Song.* Even while I was gone, she worked on the lyrics, the same as if I'd been at her side. It's like she's a part of me and now that we're truly near, I can breathe again.

And it's in that perfect moment when everything falls apart.

ZINNIA

One second, I'm chatting with Rhodes. The next thing I know, the air is filled with small red dots, like the fluff from a thousand blood-colored dandelions. The air is so thick with the stuff, I can't even see my hand in front of my face.

Magic.

The small dots flare with light. Now, they don't look like dandelion fluff so much anymore. Instead they seem exactly like the red stars that make up Pandora's starfall.

Uh oh.

Just thinking about that starfall makes my throat tight. This isn't just any magic. I think back to my talk with Kaps. Could this be something from Pandora's box? Kaps said Pandora's box brings back a dragon ghost. Now, it seems like Pandora's box is filling the air with a spell. Who know it could so that?

Around me, the haze of red thins a little. I can see again. And what I see makes me gasp. Someone steps into the courtyard.

Killian.

One red spot settles against my throat and stings me. This is definitely from Pandora's box, and it's causing trouble. I set my hand on my neck, trying to wipe off the magic. It doesn't work.

My knees go all wobbly. Killian's grumbly voice sounds in my mind.

Rest, my dragons.

I crumple onto my side. Sleep dims my mind. Killian strolls across the courtyard. With each step, red spots whirl in great loops behind him. Killian pauses by LT. A look of pure hatred tightens the Master Dragon's face. Leaning down, Killian picks up LT's tail with his thumb and forefinger, as if my friend got covered in disease.

"You know why we call you scrubs?" asks Killian.

If I weren't so sleepy, I'd gasp. You're not supposed to call part-human shifters *scrubs*. It's mean.

A long silence follows. I wait for someone to yell at Killian, yelling him to leave LT alone. But that doesn't happen. The truth appears. These little red dots must have bitten into everyone. My family is totally passed out. So are LT and his parents.

I might be the only one awake. *Yipes.*

Killian drops LT's tail. "We call you scrubs because you can scrub at your tail all day long, yet you'll never lose the pattern that marks you as part human."

LT lays collapsed onto his side. A lock of dark hair curls over his sweet face. Killian leans in closer. "I have another theory. We call you scrubs because we must erase you from existence. You don't belong here, taking up the same space as true Furor."

LT keeps sleeping peacefully. I try to yell at Killian, but the sound gets caught in my throat.

"Now die, little scrub," says Killian. Reaching into his jacket pocket, Killian pulls out a small glass cube. He then presses the container's sides in a special rhythm. The cube expands until it fits his entire palm. Soon it's a glass container with a bright red starfall pattern glowing on its sides. My blood freezes.

That's not just any cube. I was right when I saw the star pattern around me. This isn't just any magic.

It's Pandora's box.

Killian opens the top. More bright spots fly out from inside. Those glowing red points fly over to LT and cover his face like a mask. Shock twists down my spine.

There are no holes left for LT to breathe.

My friend twitches, pulling at the stuff covering his face. He's in an enchanted sleep, but even then, LT's body knows to fight being suffocated. Yet no matter how hard LT tries, the mask doesn't come off. My heart thuds against my rib cage.

Killian is smothering LT to death.

Somehow I force my eyes to stay open. There must be a way I can help LT. Killian's voice sounds in my head once more.

Rest, my dragons.

The others may sleep, but I won't. LT lays only a few yards away. I must do something.

That's when I remember what Mum said.

There's magic in my music. With whatever strength I have left, I think about *Our Song*. LT and I just shared that tune. Power lay within it. I force the words into my mind.

Gray or green or brown or yellow
Your look could change just like the rainbow

New energy moves through my veins. The magic is working. I get up on my hands and knees. It's only possible as long as I focus on *Our Song*. Just ahead, LT now pulls frantically at the red stuff covering his face. His skin turns blue. I crawl closer.

Five feet separate us.

Four.

A new figure stands above LT. It's Titan. *Yes!* LT's dad woke up. The guy looks as wobbly as I feel, but at least he's walking around. Titan leans over, ready to pull the evil spell off his son.

Killian slams into Titan instead. I can no longer see either of them.

In the distance, I hear the clash of bodies. Lightning flashes around the courtyard. Red fluff whirls nearby like a tornado. No question what's happening now. There's a battle going on. But I can't think about any of that.

I simply must save LT.

Inch by inch, I crawl toward my friend.

Three feet.

Two.

I'm close enough now. It's an effort to lift my arm, but I grit my teeth and make it happen. My fingers numbly pull at the red stuff covering LT's face while my thoughts stay focused on *Our Song.*

> *I wouldn't care*
> *It's what we share*
> *You're mine*

Suddenly, LT's red mask feels like so much cotton under my hands. I tear the coverings away from LT's nose and mouth. He sucks in a deep gasp and coughs.

I exhale. It happened. I saved LT.

Crack!

A dozen lightning bolts flash across the courtyard, more than ever before. Fresh footsteps sound nearby. Someone new has just arrived.

CRACK!

A thick web of lightning fills the air. It's more brightness than I ever thought possible. When the lightning vanishes, it takes the red stuff with it as well. The courtyard turns silent. Worry twists inside my limbs.

What happened?

I force myself to scan the scene. Everyone is still asleep, except me. Killian stands in the center of the courtyard, along with his father, Oswine. The old Master Dragon must have been the new person who joined the fight.

That's not good.

Then I see Titan. LT's father lies on the ground nearby; his chest is covered in blood. My heart cracks with sadness.

While patting Pandora's box, Killian turns to Oswine. "See? No one can withstand our power."

Oswine sniffs. "See that pattern on the outside of the box? It's less red now. You drained it." Sure enough, Pandora's box shone bright red when Killian first brought it out. Now it's faded. "Is there enough for the rest of our mission?"

My eyes widen. Rest of our mission? What's that, exactly?

"There's more than enough power for what I plan," says Killian. "Pandora's box recharges at the height of the starfall. There is plenty to finish everything that needs to be done before then." When Killian says the words, *everything that needs to be done before then*, he looks at his father in a mean way. If I were Oswine, I'd run for it.

"Good," says Oswine. The old Thorntail scans the courtyard. "So which one do we take?"

Killian inspects the courtyard, too. His gaze lands on me. "I had thought to kidnap Kaps, but Zinnia is clearly the best one here. She fought back."

I manage to croak out one word. "No."

Killian motions to Oswine. "Do you have the mortal medicine?"

"Yes," replies Oswine. The older dragon pulls a tube from his pocket. I can't miss how the thing ends with a nasty-looking needle. I've seen these before in books—humans use them use to stick medicine into each other.

Killian frowns. "And you're sure this will work?"

"You still want everyone to think she's dead, yet we secretly keep her alive for *our* purposes?" asks Oswine.

"Obviously." Killian's mouth twists into a sneery-look. "But can human medicine do what we wish? I still think we should use magic."

Now it's Oswine's turn to sneer. "If we fake-killed her with magic, then others could trace it easily. The emperor and empress would undo the spell in minutes. But this serum is from humans, not mages. No matter what spell is cast, the girl will still appear dead to them. Then we return and claim her later."

"We'll see," says Killian. "Give her the serum."

Once again, I keep thinking of *Our Song*.

Gray or green or brown or yellow
Your look could change just like a rainbow
I wouldn't care
It's what we share
You're mine

The music sends fresh power through my limbs. I stand up. "Keep away from me," I warn.

Killian chuckles. "You're very strong in magic. Perhaps too much so. Maybe we should take Kaps after all. Oswine, stick the sister."

I look to my poor twin. Kaps still lays passed out on the ground. "No!" I hobble forward. "If I let you take me, will you leave my family alone?"

Killian grins. "Of course."

I lift my chin. "Swear it with magic."

Killian opens Pandora's box. More bits of bright red fly out and land on me, Oswine, and Killian. "Per the power of Pandora, we three agree that only Zinnia shall be taken from Furonium today. In return, Zinnia agrees to serve as our Vessel for the Future. When Pandora's starfall is at its highest about eight years from now, Zinnia will then allow us to enhance her powers with the spirit of the ultimate dragon, Chimera. Do you agree?"

That's a whole lot of terrible, but if it keeps my family safe? I'm in.

"All right," I say. "Do it."

A minute ago, red bits of power settled onto me, Oswine and Killian. Now those dots glow more brightly. Sliding down my arms, they take the form of red manacles around my wrists. These are the old-time type thingies used by pirates, complete with heavy loops on metal that are connected by a chain. The manacles flare with red light before melting into my skin. I know enough about magic to realize one thing.

The spell is cast.

Oswine marches up to me, the syringe in his wrinkled old-guy hand. Seconds later, chilly metal bites into my neck. This time, my magic is helpless against the need for sleep. The last thing I see is Oswine pull out a note from his pocket and read aloud.

"To the false emperor and empress: As promised, we have killed one of your bloodline to pay for the shameful death of Chimera, the greatest dragon emperor who ever lived. Consider your debt paid. —The Triumvirate."

Oswine sets the sheet of paper on the ground beside me and laughs.

As I lose all consciousness, I make a silent vow. With whatever magic is within me, I will break this spell.

I refuse to be your vessel of anything.

6

RHODES

*M*y dreams go to strange places. Zin sings in a field of lightning bolts. I try to get my guitar and play for her, but I can't find my instrument.

Sienna's voice cuts through the haze. "Little Titan? Can you hear me?"

I open my eyes. The last thing I knew, I'd been sitting in the courtyard when red bits of light appeared all around me. Something bit into my neck; I passed out. When I woke up, I expected to see the courtyard once more.

That's not what I see.

Instead I'm inside my cottage. The place is all wooden furniture, stone walls, and photos of Sienna in concert. Cellos, guitars and sheet music lay everywhere. Someone must have dragged me in here and put me on my bed. I blink hard, forcing my eyes to focus on Sienna. She sits on the edge of the mattress. Her skin looks far more pale than normal.

Sienna exhales. "You're awake, my Little Titan."

"What happened?" I ask.

"That depends." Sienna picks at a thread on the edge of my comforter. "What's the last thing you remember?"

"Zin and I played a song for everyone. The air filled with red fluff and I passed out."

"It was a spell," explains Sienna. "Everyone else went unconscious as well, except for Zin and Titan."

"I told you, Zin's really powerful in magic." I glance toward the closed door. Surely, Zin's somewhere nearby and worrying about me. I need to find her.

Zin, where are you?

"Your face was covered in a spell," explains Sienna. "That's why it took you longer to wake up. The Kathikon brought you in here to recover. There was a note from the Triumvirate..." Sienna tears up. *My mother is crying.* Every nerve in my body goes on edge.

"What else happened?" I ask.

"The Triumvirate killed Zinnia."

"No." I sit bolt upright. "There must be some way to heal Zin."

"Don't you think we all tried? The emperor and empress are strong in magic; they worked over Zinnia's body for hours. She's gone, Little Titan. There's nothing more that magic can do. Zinnia will take her place her in the royal tombs tonight."

My limbs go numb. I know it's royal custom to bury people quickly. That thought never bothered me before. But now? This is Zin we're talking about. There must be something we can do. I want more time.

"When do they bury her?" I ask.

"Two hours from now." Sienna covers her mouth. She's holding in a sob.

My skin prickles over with worry. Zinnia dying wouldn't be enough to upset Sienna this way. "There's more," I say. "Tell me."

Sienna shivers. "It's awful, my Little Titan."

The way Sienna says *my Little Titan* makes my heart sink. If my body felt numb before, now it's like I'm outside my own form. I float by the ceiling, watching a catastrophe hit some other version of LT. I swallow hard and force the next words from my mouth. "Where's Father?"

"He fought the Triumvirate," says Sienna. She bows her head. Tears drip from her nose onto the comforter.

I stand. "Where is he, Sienna?"

"Our bedroom."

While my head stays stuck in that dreamlike state, I'm somehow able to walk out the door. Sienna doesn't follow. In a way, that confirms my worst suspicions. I march into my parents' bedroom. Father is laid out on the bed. His chest is torn open.

He's dead.

My body seems to crumple on its own. Next thing I know, I kneel at Father's bedside. Reaching forward, I take Titan's hand in mine. It's cold as snow. Father was always filled with strength and determination. Now he's lifeless. I set his chilly palm against my cheek and weep.

Both Titan and Zin are gone.

And so, part of me dies as well.

7

ZINNIA

*W*hen I wake up, I find myself resting on a really cold mattress. I try to move. That doesn't happen. Not at first, anyway. Eventually I'm able to open my eyes.

Huh.

My mind is foggy, but I can still remember the red party dress I'm wearing. It's one of my favorites. So that's good. Sadly, the rest of what I see doesn't make any sense.

For starters, this isn't a mattress.

I'm on a stone table thingy. Flowers surround me. The walls are also made of gray rock. A shiver runs up my back. I know what this place is: *my family's tomb*. It's a long stone building that stands in a back corner of the palace grounds. I only peeked in once and that was on a dare from Kaps. Inside, the tomb is filled with these table-thingies that have skeletons on top.

Now, there's me.

This is really really REALLY bad.

What's going on? There must be a reason for all this. My head still seems stuck in a haze. If I focus really hard, I can remember Oswine shooting something into my neck. Is that why I'm so out of it?

Or is this a trick from Kaps?

That's much more likely.

Last month, I locked Kaps in the royal compost shack right after the servants dumped a bunch of horse poop in there. My twin promised to get me back. That could be what's happening now.

Yeah, that has to be it. Kaps.

Some of the bigger bunches of flowers have signs on them. If I squint super-hard, I can read what they say.

Condolences
All our love
Best wishes

Okay, this is a little weird. *Condolences.* That's a gown-up word for *sorry.* Is Kaps apologizing for putting me in a tomb? I scan more of the flowers. When I see one particular sign, it sends new chills through me.

We'll Miss You, Princess Zinnia

More of the mist leaves my head. This isn't a joke from Kaps. I remember now. Oswine explained it before.

This serum is from humans, not mages. No matter what spell is cast, the girl will still appear dead to them. Then we return and claim her later.

The Triumvirate made me look dead, so my family put me in the royal tomb. Next Killian and Oswine will show up to *claim me,* whatever that means.

No doubt, it's nothing good.

I must get out of here.

Another memory appears. The courtyard. LT was choking. To save him, I used our music—our beat—to access my magic.

Maybe that can help me now. Closing my eyes, I remember the words for *Our Song.*

Gray or green or brown or yellow
Your look could change just like a rainbow

My leg twitches. *Yes!* Progress.

I keep focusing on the music. Soon I'm able to shift my entire right arm. I'm feeling pretty good when two figures step up to my tomb-table. It's Killian and Oswine. *Yipes.* I'd hoped to sneak out before anyone evil got here.

"She's waking up," says Killian. He holds a glass container in his hands. I recognize that thing right away: Pandora's box.

"See," says Oswine. "I told you it would work."

Killian holds the box up to the light. "There should be plenty of magic left for what we ned to do."

Oswine frowns. "But we're just locking her up until Pandora's starfall is at its height. Why would you need to cast more spells?"

"Because I disagree with your plan."

"We've been through this before," grumbles Oswine. "You openly rule the Thorntails. I secretly lead the Triumvirate." He points at me. "This one goes into a hidden dungeon for a little over eight years. No magic needed."

"Ah," says Killian slowly. "In that case, I think we should test Pandora's box. See if it really can summon a ghost."

Oswine's beady eyes widen. "Do you mean?"

"Let's call forth Chimera and place his power in you."

Oswine frowns. "I thought that would only work on the day the starfall is at its height."

"It will work *best* on that day, certainly," says Killian.

"And don't I need to be from Chimera's bloodline for my body to accept the ghost?" asks Oswine.

Killian takes a half-step backward. "Who found the sacred

scrolls that show how to command Pandora's box? Me. I shall place the soul of Chimera into you and then remove it right away. Believe me, it is more than possible. Imagine … the three dragon heads of Chimera, each holding a different power … and they are all in you."

Oswine scans the massive tomb. "I could shift into his dragon form?"

"That's for you to discover," says Killian. "Don't you want to experience that power, just once?"

Oswine nods quickly. "Yes, it would be an honor."

Now, if I could talk I'd say, *getting stuffed with my evil grandpa is a dumb idea.* But I can't say a word. In this situation, that may not be a bad thing.

"Perfect." Killian opens the glass container. "Per the power of Pandora's box, I hereby summon the spirit of Chimera, the greatest dragon emperor of all time. I demand that the ghost of Chimera enter the body of Oswine of the Thorntails." Killian looks to his father. "Do you agree?"

"Yes," says Oswine. "I consent."

Red points of light rise up from inside the box. The bright bits pour out onto the floor and twirl around Oswine's body.

Oswine tries to straighten his crooked shoulders. "I welcome thee, oh Chimera!"

The red haze around Oswine grows heavier, twisting about the old guy like mummy wrappings. Little by little, those bright bits seep inside Oswine's body. All the time, the old dude looks totally blissed out.

Now, I'm partly frozen and laying on a stone table, but even I know this won't end well.

"It is done," cries Oswine. "I can sense the power of the three-headed dragon inside me!"

Suddenly, all the magical stuff within Oswine seeps to the surface again. His skin glows red. A sinister smile curls across Oswine's mouth. "I am Chimera. I shall rise again."

That's not just Oswine with Chimera's powers. Not at all. That's an old dude who's now possessed by my evil grandfather.

A low rumble fills the air. The new mortal Chimera-Oswine combo vibrates in place. The movement is so intense, he looks blurry. Long seconds tick by.

Chimera-Oswine explodes.

Little bits of nasty old guy fly everywhere. It's super disgusting. At least, nothing gets in my mouth. After a few moments, all the chunks-o-Oswine vanish.

Good riddance, I say.

Killian stares at the mist for a long moment. "Oh no," he says at last. "Seems I forgot. You're were exactly right, Father. Pandora's box will only permanently merge a ghost into a dragon at the height of the starfall. That's when there's enough power to make the spell stick. You can't stay as one with Chimera."

Killian sets his hand to his ear, as if hearing someone else speak. "What's that you say, Father? You wish to know why you exploded? That would be my other miss on my part. Turns out, you do need to be from Chimera's bloodline not to implode with this spell. Oops. Now it appears I must rule both the Thorntails and the Triumvirate."

Killian turns to me. "Let's discuss what happens next. You're to become part of a special training program for Thorntails."

I force out three words. "Not ... a ... Thorntail."

"We'll fix that. You'll also receive your instruction at a unique area on Earth that I've selected."

More forcing-out words. "I'll ... escape."

"I shall fix that as well."

"Won't ... do ... what ... you ... want."

"Your lack of motivation has already been addressed." Killian snaps his fingers; a set of magical red manacles appear on my wrists.

I tilt my head. Memories knock around at the back of my brain, but I can't recall them clearly. "What are these things?"

"I was about to kidnap Kaps," says Killian. "Your sister would then have been our Vessel for the Future. But you promised to take her place. We cast a spell on the deal. Those manacles are the sign of that incantation. There's no running away from this, little Zinnia."

My skin prickles over.

Memories appear.

Oh, no. Killian is right.

Killian reopens Pandora's box once more. "Per the power of Pandora's box, I order this girl be limited with a cuff of binding." Red spots rise from the container. The bright bits fill the room, just like they'd expanded through the air in the courtyard.

Then they all whiz toward me.

All I can sense is red blur around me. The electric charge of magic fills the air. The red spots merge into two objects. One is a crystal ball that hovers right by my chest. The other is a red cuff that fits about the end of my tail, right before the arrowhead shaped end.

This is bonkers.

Not sure what I expected would happen, but a crystal ball and tail cuff wasn't it. The crystal ball is something Furor use at fairs to tell your fortune. And a tail cuff is just jewelry. What do they want me to do? Join the circus and as the magical jewelry-girl with a crystal ball following her around?

Killian points at my tail. "Once activated, that cuff will alter your tail's color. Tails with black scales tails mean royalty. Yours will look gray, like the Thorntail tribe. You are part of our special training program, after all."

I slip off the table thingy. "Whatever you say." It seems like Killian is the chatty type. And people make mistakes with spells all the time. Maybe I can still escape. My parents can break whatever spells Killian put on me.

"The cuff does more than that," says Killian. "It will also limit your movements to the training area."

I inch toward the door. The crystal ball thingy still floats in front of my chest. *That's awkward.* "And this crystal ball?"

"It will erase your personal memories. Once I snap my fingers, both spells will activate."

"I'll forget everything?" I pause. "Even my family? LT?"

"Absolutely." Killian grins. "You'll also forget that I'm Furor. My tail will vanish from your sight alone."

Anger spins through me. "You're lying. My magic is too strong. I won't forget anything, especially who *you* are."

"We'll see," says Killian. He snaps her fingers. The cuff on my tail and the crystal ball flare with red light. I scan my memories. I know my name. Zinnia. And my parents. Even LT.

I was right. This didn't work.

The tail cuff blares with red light once more. Even more brightness dances within the crystal ball that hovers before me. Cords of red light now pour out of my forehead and into the crystal ball. Along each thread, I can see images flicker inside. There's Ma and Da. My sisters. The palace. LT.

My memories are being stolen.

The crystal ball flares more brightly than ever before, then it slams into my chest. The spell actually merges inside me. Red specks take over my sight. My legs turn rubbery as I fall to the ground. Even so, I don't give up.

My magic is strong enough to break this. I won't do what Killian wants. Ever.

8

RHODES

I stand at edge of Wineton Sea. The churning red waters stretch out toward the horizon. Overhead, Pandora's starfall arches across a darkened sky. The sight reminds me of so many tears.

Was it only last night that we placed Zin in her family's tomb? Feels like a year ago. And now, the funeral ceremony for Father is about to begin. I stand at the head of a long line of Electrophus dragons. Behind me waits my uncle Atlas. The row stretches far off along the black sand beach. I think almost every dragon in our tribe is here to show their respects. Knowing that helps a little.

Off to my left stand the sacred workers. They donate time for services like this one. All wear red togas. The Electrophus tribe are a sea people. We were the first to make contact with any humans. In our case, it was the ancient Greeks. Today all tribes uses Greek letters in our names. That's Electrophus.

On my right wait all the non-tribal mourners. There's my mother and some of her human friends. The imperial family stand on the beach as well: the emperor, empress, Kaps and Huntress. They're wearing their formal get-up, complete with crowns. Father kept them safe; it means a lot that they're here so soon after Zin's burial.

Atlas sets his hand on my shoulder. He's my father's brother, all right. Same green skin. Same hefty touch.

"Yes, uncle?" I ask.

"It is time," says Atlas.

Nodding, I strip off my T-shirt and jeans. Per Electrophus tradition, we must enter the water in order to bury our dead.

And no Electrophus enters the deep in human form.

As I wade forward, the sand gives way to tiny stones beneath my feet. I partially change from human to dragon. My skin covers over with green scales. Talons appear on my fingers. All of a sudden, it strikes me as a shame that regular humans can't see our dragon side. They can't even see our tails. For once, I'd like for Sienna to witness all the dragons who celebrate Father.

She won't, though.

When I get deep enough into the water, I fully change into my dragon form. I'm a massive and sleek beast. Horns encircle my head. Heavy plates spike down my back. I dive into the water and swim out toward the deep. As I move along, electric eels keep pace with me. These are animal familiars of our tribe. Something in my chest unfurls to have them near.

A deep cavern opens up in the ocean floor. This is it. The place for the ceremony. I pause beside the massive hole and wait. More dragons follow until we create a kind of column around the great round pit down below. Second pass. The whoosh of water sounds in my ears. Gentle liquid streams across my scales.

Then I see it.

Far above, a thin slash of white bobs on the ocean's surface. *A boat.* And not just any vessel, but Father's funeral barge.

It's my role to start the process of tearing it apart.

Within my chest, magic churns. It's the power of my people. An image appears in my mind: it's me and Zin singing our last song as Father stands nearby. The music pounds through my soul, churning up more supernatural power.

As Atlas said, *it is time.*

Leaning back my head, I open my great dragon jaws. Bolts of lightning shoot past my teeth and slam into the boat's hull. Beside me, Atlas opens his mouth as well. More lightning pierces the boat. Soon, every dragon makes his own lightning-offering into Father's funeral barge. The red sea dances with this brightness.

I'm not sure how long we blast at Father's boat. At some point, my soul starts to feel empty. I close my jaws and end the lightning. All other dragons do the same. Overhead, there's no sign of father's boat anymore. We incinerated it as a tribe.

The ceremony is over.

I'm first to make my way back to shore. The rest of my tribe follows. As I swim along, it strikes me that most of the time, there's so little separating those of us who are part human ... from others who are all Furor. Some colored scales on the bottom of our tails. That's it.

But for such a little difference, both my father and Zin are dead.

The water grows more shallow. I transform into my partial-dragon form. Green scales shine where other mortals would have skin. My tail swipes behind me. Horns still jut out around my head. As I step onto the black sand, a sacred worker hands me a fresh red toga. I slip it on and with that, the ceremony is over. I now fully change back to my human form.

Electrophus ceremonies have no long speeches or anything. We each give our offering of lightning to the deceased. That's it. I nod toward the emperor and empress. They bow their heads in my direction. Some part of me says I should step over and thank them for coming. But every inch of my body feels drained after the ceremony. Making small talk with royalty is off the list.

And there's also the weight of guilt in my bones.

How could I have done nothing while Zin was killed?

I march over to Sienna. She wears a red robe, same as the rest of the tribe. She forces a smile as I approach. "It was beautiful. We saw all the lightning from here."

"That's good." At least, she can see the lightning, if not the dragons.

Sienna gazes toward the sky. "The starfall looks different tonight."

Sometimes Sienna and I think the same way. I know what she means here. Sienna touches my shoulder. It's a gentle brush of her fingers but for her, that's a lot. And there's no question what it means. She knows I saw the sky crying, same as she did.

Atlas steps up to Sienna and me. "Greetings, Sienna. LT."

"Call me Rhodes. That's my dragon name." The moment the words leave my mouth, I know they're right. I'm not Little Titan any more. After all, how can I be when there's no big Titan left?

Atlas nods. "As you prefer."

Sienna pins me with a fierce stare. For a moment, I think she's about to tell me that I should stay LT forever. Then she shakes her head. "Rhodes it is."

"There's something I wish to discuss with you both," says Atlas.

"Go on," says Sienna.

"Rhodes must take over guarding the princesses," states Atlas.

This is obvious. "Of course," I say. Then I catch the shocked look on Sienna's face. Maybe this was no question to me, but it seems to surprise my mother.

Sienna shivers. "Isn't Rhodes too young?"

"Guarding is suitable work for children in our tribe, as long as a mentor is present. I'll be at his side."

Sienna rounds on me. "No more music then?"

"No more music," I confirm. *Without Zin, there's no point.*

Sienna's mouth falls open. For a few seconds, she grinds out silent words. Then my mother straightens her shoulders. "As you wish, Rhodes. Acting as royal guard would have made Titan proud." She turns to watch the starfall before stepping away.

Guess that conversation is over.

For a long minute, Atlas and I watch my mother walk away. It seems like I should follow her, maybe wrap her in a hug or something. But Sienna was never the embracing type.

Atlas breaks the silence. "It's not your fault, you know."

"Sienna?" I ask.

"No, Zinnia."

How I wish I could believe that. That's what I'd like to say. Instead I hold my tongue. In a move like my father, I just change the subject. "What do you make of the princesses?"

"Huntress can care for herself." My uncle nods toward Kaps. "You'll have trouble with the other one, though."

Kaps catches us looking at her. She bounds away from her family to approach me and Atlas. Kaps has donned a red party dress, just like what Zin wore that last day. Kaps smiles, but the grin looks forced. That's when I know the truth.

Kaps feels guilty about Zin, same as I do.

The princess marches up, stops before me and sets her fists on her hips. I've seen this move from Kaps before. She's got some big news to share. Sure enough, Kaps lifts her chin and makes her big announcement. "I can sing too, you know," she says.

Of all the things I expected Kaps to say, this wasn't on the list. What's this girl up to anyway? Before replying, I work keep my features carefully neutral. Music training wasn't the only thing I've studied in my life. Father taught me how to act around someone I'm guarding.

"Singing," I say. "That's good."

"We should form a band together," Kaps continues. "We can use the music as a cover. The band will tour Earth while we *really* search for magical stuff. I heard there's a lot of Furor treasure hidden outside our realm."

Atlas narrows his eyes. "You've been listening to rumors

about L'Griffe. They're renegade dragons who cause us no end of trouble on Earth. Don't tangle with them."

"Why should I worry?" asks Kaps. "I'll have LT in my band."

"Rhodes. My name is Rhodes. And I'm not playing music any more."

"Fine, Rhodes. You can just protect us." With that, Kaps marches away.

"Like I told you," says Atlas. "She'll give you trouble." He rubs his chin slowly, his eyes lost in thought. "Do you expect her parents will go along with this *band idea?*"

"Yeah, I do."

The emperor and empress will get what Kaps is trying here, the same as I do. Kaps thinks that if the music goes on, then it's like Zin isn't dead. Somehow, I don't think it will work that way. But I can't quite summon up the strength to take on Kaps about it. She looks too much like Zin and not, all at once. The only real differences are their hair and eye colors.

It's enough to tear your heart out, mostly because I'm certain that Zin was my rhana. We Furor only get one life mate.

And I've lost mine forever.

9

ZINNIA

I wake up in a very huge and dark cave while wearing a red dress. This is both shocking and something I expected.

Strange.

Sitting up, I scope out the gagillion-yard cavern around me. It's all dark shadows and rough stone. Standard cave stuff.

A man waits nearby. To me, adults come in two flavors: grown-up and really old. This guy is definitely a grown-up. He's got grayish skin, black hair that's combed back, and a puffy face. His outfit is a gray suit that's way too small for him. Even through I can't see a tail, I'm pretty sure this man is Furor.

"What's your name?" he asks.

I sit upright. My thoughts whir through his question. What's my name? Abigail, Janice, something else? No answer appears. With that realization, my body turns numb.

"I don't know my name," I say slowly.

"I'm Killian." He waves his hand in a 'get over here' motion. Fifty or so humans—both male and female—step out from the shadows of this massive cave. "These are my followers. Your handlers. They are here for your protection."

All the mortals wear black body armor. Fake tails have been painted onto their butts and legs. Meanwhile, real rage demons curl across their chests. Not that humans can see rage demons. I can, though. They're oversized lizards whose bellies are covered in needles. Some demons latch on to good people and turn then bad. Rage demons aren't like that. When you carry anger in your heart, rage demons jump on and make it worse.

Even so, what are mortals doing here while wearing painted-on tails? That's a Furor thing, and dragon shifters are supposed to be secret.

"Humans shouldn't know about us," I say. Odd that I can't remember my own name but I do know this.

"These aren't any mortals, they are your handlers." Killian sighs. "You are the last of our kind, the Furor."

I give him the side-eye. "You look pretty healthy to me."

Killian steps closer and angles to one side. *I was wrong.* He doesn't have a tail, painted or otherwise.

"As you can see," declares Killian "I am human, too. Your handlers and I will build you into the greatest Furor who ever lived. And with your boosted magic, you will raise our people from the dead."

"Me? I'm a just a kid."

"No, you are the Vessel of our Future."

I frown. This whole scene looks fishy to me. There's this overly big cave … humans marching in from the shadows … this not-a-Furor guy saying I'm some Vessel of the Future. It's a lot of drama.

"Why can't I remember anything?" I ask.

"You knew about humans and Furor."

"Fine." I huff out a breath. "Why can't I remember anything *personal*?"

"You are the sacred Vessel of the Future. Specific memories will only hinder your preparation. By keeping your mind clean, you will be ready."

"For what, exactly?" This guy talks in riddles. It's annoying.

"When Pandora's starfall is at its brightest, then you will gain the powers of the greatest dragon of us all." Killian gives me a nasty smile. "I checked, and the starfall will be brightest on your eighteenth birthday. Isn't that nice gift?"

"If you say so." *Wow. I have no idea what he's talking about.*

"For the next eight-plus years, you will learn to answer to me and only me."

I rise and brush the dirt off my skirt. "I refuse. Now how do I get out of here?"

"You can't deny this. You made a magical vow."

Red manacles materialize on my wrists. *Magic.* The image of a crystal ball appears in my mind. In the depths of the red glass, I see a Furor girl laying on the ground.

I had to save her.

With that, I know the truth. *What Killian says is right.* I did make some kind of magical promise and saved that girl. Now if only I could see her face, then we'd be getting somewhere.

Killian grins. "You know I am correct."

I nod and stare at the sand. The manacles disappear from my wrists. My internal vision of the crystal ball vanishes as well. I straighten my back. *So I have enchanted manacles and a crystal ball vision thingy following me around. That's only magic.* All spells have backdoors. I just need to find one here.

Killian paces a line before me. "You'll begin intensive training immediately. It will cover fighting, mental acuity and history. Later, when you become super-powered, then you will have all the skills you need to bring back our people."

That crystal ball reappears in my mind. Many faces flicker through its center. Somehow I know another truth. "I have family."

"And they must be kept safe," says Killian. "But to do that, you need to forget them for a while. Focus on your studies. Develop perfect memory. Which reminds me... Come forward." Killian waves his arm. An older lady in gray robes steps out from behind the wall of humans. She's got a wrinkled face, tanned skin and kind eyes. "This is Grace. She'll be a special kind of handler for you: a tutor. The other handlers will serve as sparring partners and guards."

The older lady bows her head. "Greetings, oh Vessel of the Future."

Killian keeps staring at me with his beady eyes. "With Grace's help, you shall rescue our people."

He's hitting that rescue stuff really hard. "And I have to stay in this cave?"

"You have twenty miles of desert in which to roam. That tail cuff will keep you to the boundaries."

My tail knows when it's the topic of discussion. It swoops around to arch before me. Sure enough, there's a red cuff right by the arrowhead end. This is so weird, but maybe if I keep this guy talking, he'll share something useful.

I tap my tail cuff. "Okay."

"And you'll need to shift into your dragon form. Human shape is disgusting. Then your handlers and I will give you a tour of your new home."

"But shifting will ruin my pretty red dress." I fluff the skirts to show the loveliness better. That's when I feel it.

A book.

It's in my pocket.

And I want to keep it.

"Fine," I say quickly. "I'll change into a dragon and shred the dress along the way. But you and all your handlers must go outside."

"Why?" asks Killian.

I say the first thing that comes into my head. "I'm shy."

Killian sniffs. "That's not how shifters are and you know it."

I fold my arms over my chest. "You said my personal memories are gone so I can better train. Right?"

Killian narrows his eyes. "Yes."

"Then my shyness is still here because it serves some purpose for me to become the best Vessel of the Future ever. All of you…" I point to Killian and the handlers. "Outside. Now."

Killian stares at me for a long minute. It feels like we've swapped roles. Now he knows I'm lying about something but he can't tell what it is, either.

Good.

After what feels like a hundred years, Killian swipes his hand through the air again. "Fall out, handlers."

Everyone marches out of the cave. Once they're totally gone, I quickly bury my book and cover up the spot with some fallen bits of rock.

Perfect. Totally hidden.

Next I summon my dragon form. A little bit of white light flares under my skin as I transform into a long gray dragon. I take in a deep breath, expecting something to burn in my stomach.

Fire maybe?

I scan my scales. Still gray. That means I'm Thorntail tribe. Why would I expect to breathe fire? I shake off the thought. With so much strangeness happening today, the question of why I'd expect to breathe fire seems silly.

With my transformation complete, I crawl toward the cave mouth. After a few yards, I pause. Should I really do this? Clearly, I did make a vow of some kind. That's why I've got enchanted manacles for crying out loud. But I'm also sure that Killian is a lying liar.

Pawing at the sandy ground, I think through my options. There aren't many. My best bet is to follow Killian and get more information. Then I'll figure out a plan.

After all, I do remember one thing. Magic is already inside me.

I just need to figure out how to wield it and escape.

PRESENT DAY

ZINNIA, AGE SEVENTEEN

another day outside with Gracie.

Officially, Gracie is supposed to stand in the sun all day. Yet she's an old human who must wear heavy gray robes. The poor lady sweats up a storm. *Which makes sense.* The desert outside my cave is rather uncomfortable for humans. That's one reason why I stay in dragon form all the time. My mortal handlers—the ones with the rage demons on their chests—just finished their hourly sweep. After they left, I conjured up a chair and umbrella by my cave entrance.

Gracie deserves some comfort.

After all, Gracie's presence is the only thing that makes my desert life bearable. A chair and umbrella are the least I can do for her. And sadly, it's the most I can do with my magic here.

Gracie closes her eyes. "Let us review thy lesson for the day."

Laying on my dragon's belly, I set my massive chin against the sand. "That is acceptable." When I first got here, I thought Gracie spoke strangely. Now her words seem natural. And since the other handlers don't speak to me so much as grunt and gesture—and then only during our battle practices—Gracie is my only company.

She is a fine companion.

"What made the Prussian military superior?" asks Gracie.

"Which era?"

"Let us say, the mid-1800's."

That is simple. "Aggression. They always went for the kill."

"You discount their training?" asks Gracie. She always pushes me to think versus memorize things.

"They train to be aggressive," I counter. "Move quickly. Fight fiercely. Encircle the enemy. Next question."

Gracie chuckles. "Well spoken, oh Vessel of the Future." A bead of sweat glistens as it runs down her cheek. My poor tutor. In my dragon form, the desert is all things warm and comfortable. I rarely shift to a human state.

"Now I shall ask thy next question," says Gracie.

"Go on."

Gracie does all her lessons from memory. Books are not allowed in my training grounds. I only learn things verbally, either from Gracie or from the chatter of my handlers when they do not think I can hear them.

"When you gain the power of Chimera, what shall you do?"

"Repair the Furor world."

"Be more specific."

I flip my dragon's gaze onto Gracie. My pupils flare red with demonic power. "We both know the truth, Gracie. Whatever Killian has planned, I do not exist after Friday." That's my birthday. Six days from now.

"You don't know that. I haven't spent this many years teaching you just to lose you."

So that's what this is about. "I get flashes of memory, Gracie. Sometimes I see an old man's face transform into skin that seems more red stone than flesh. He speaks with a voice that is not his own. I believe that is someone changing into Chimera. It is a warning. I must find a way to escape, Gracie. That is my only chance."

A scent wafts on the air. Foul feet and vinegar. Killian is coming.

"The Son of Oswine is on his way," I warn.

Gracie hops up to stand. She cannot be seen as lounging. It's time to hide her comforts—I do not wish my Gracie to get in trouble.

Closing my eyes, I think of a few random scraps of music. It's how I activate my magic. It's also forbidden. Gracie can teach me nothing musical. And my handlers are forbidden to speak to me, let alone sing.

Yet I remember bits of tunes here and there. Now, I pull one into my mind. It's something about blossoms and rainbows. Sure enough, an electric sense fills the air. Magic.

Now to cast the spell.

As I keep the tune in mind, I picture Gracie's chair and umbrella vanishing into the sand. Moments later, those two items vibrate in place. My magic encircles them in a haze that resembles heat rising from the desert. The chair and umbrella shimmy for a moment longer. Next they burrow under the sand.

Gone.

Vanished.

Perfect.

Now, if only I could access enough magic to break the spells on my tail cuff. Or the crystal ball that holds my memories. And let us not forget the biggest enchantment of all: the red bindings that hold me to my vow.

Ah, well. I still have time. Not very much of it, but some.

A quarter mile from my cavern there rises a great sand dune. The ground gently thrums with the footsteps of many humans. Soon they crest the dune: my fifty human handlers with Killian standing at their center. As always, the handlers wear their black armor with painted-on tails. Killian still crams his mighty form into a small gray suit.

Moving as one, the group marches down the dune. I do not

bother to sit up. Killian visits every week at this time for my so-called inspection. It is tedious, although sometimes I do get to hunt demons as part of this ritual. That can be enjoyable.

Killian pauses before me. Sunlight glints off the container in his hands. Pandora's box. Humans stand in neat rows behind him. My handlers.

Killian bows his head. "Greetings, oh Vessel of the Future."

"Greetings, oh Son of Oswine."

Moving in unison, the humans collapse onto one knee. "We greet thee, oh Vessel." It's one of the few things they say to me directly.

"You may rise." Unless I speak those words, my handlers will kneel there all day.

"It is time for your weekly inspection," states Killian.

With that statement, I force myself to sit up. If I don't seem alert during the actual inspection, it results in a lot of whining and worry. *Am I backing off on my promise to become the vessel? Is my attitude turning sour?*

We've been over this, time and again. In my mind, I repeat the phrases that helped me survive all these years.

I gave my promise. It is magically binding. I shall make good on my vow... until I find a way to break it.

Killian raises Pandora's box. I scan the star pattern on the container's surface. The box doesn't hold unlimited magic. It must be refilled each time Pandora's starfall is at its height. In other words, once every thousand years. Killian used to be careful with the magic inside. The star pattern stayed bright for ages. But lately, he's been getting careless. Gracie told me he even used a bunch of magic to cast a love spell that failed anyway. These days, the star pattern is barely visible—some faint pink marks and that is all.

Which is good. It means Killian has perhaps one last spell

stored inside Pandora's box and that is all. This will make it easier for me to escape.

"You're almost ready," announces Killian. "When Pandora's starfall at its height, there will be enough power for me to enhance you with the full abilities of Chimera. The starfall date falls on your birthday. What a present, eh?"

"As you say," I reply. Killian states this birthday fact every week. It lost any sting years ago.

"State your purpose," says Killian.

I heave in a slow breath. This is another ritual between us. Best to get it over with quickly. "I am the last of my kind," I begin. "When Pandora's starfall is at its height, I shall become super-powered with the abilities of Chimera, the greatest dragon emperor of all. Then I shall rebuild the Furor world and return our families to life."

Of all the words in this statement, there is only one part I like: *return our families to life.*

I recall nothing about my past. But somehow, I'm certain I have a family somewhere. Sometimes an image appears in my mind. A crystal ball. Hazy figures move inside the orb.

They are my family; I know it.

That crystal ball is both my comfort and pain. It reminds me of my vow and shows glimpses of my family. My history is trapped in there, yet I can't access any of it.

One day, I'll best that crystal ball and get my memories back. Trouble is, I'm running out of time.

Killian steeples his hefty fingers under his chin. "The transformation is six days away. Are you ready?"

"I am," I reply. It is surprising how calm I sound. Inside, I am screaming.

"Show me," states Killian.

I know what he's wondering about. "Bring me an opponent." Sometimes, Killian captures a demon or two and forces me to fight them. Lately, this has been happening every week. It take it as another sign of Killian growing wasteful with magic as my birthday approaches. Why save power when it will all be replenished soon?

"Fine," says Killian. The gleam in his eye says he already cast a spell for this occasion. It's what he always does. "Vessel of the Future, meet a few demons from today."

Before me, the sand churns. Hisses sound as a pair of blood lions tear up through the ground. They have red fur with bat wings. Their eyes gleam with demonic power. The two demons claw at the sand. Their movements have a rhythm all its own. I focus on that music, not that I'll tell the others about this.

1, 2, 3... 1, 2, 3... the blood lions pace around me in a slow beat.

Perfect.

Time to fight.

ZINNIA

The world collapses into the pair of blood lions. All I know is my enemies. The first is small, wiry, and fast. She'll strike right away and try to wear me down. The second is larger and heavier; she'll go in for the kill.

They continue to pace in a line before me.

1, 2, 3… 1, 2, 3…

With each step, these lion-shaped demons grow larger. Within a dozen paces, the pair are dragon-sized, the same as me. I scan the second one more closely. She's perhaps even larger than my dragon form.

That is good. I enjoy a fine fight.

The larger one unfurls her wings. Interesting. So, the big blood lion demon wishes to go first. Fine. I brace myself, setting my forelegs deeper in the sand.

She does not attack me, though.

Instead, the larger demon leaps toward Gracie. In a single smooth movement, the big blood lion snaps her jaws around the back of Gracie's robes. Panic zings though my limbs as Gracie fights to get loose from her garment. Yet the bite is too tight. My beloved tutor can't get free.

Spreading her wings, the larger blood lion takes to the air. The smaller demon does the same.

My mind records every aspect of this moment. The terror on Gracie's sweet face as she rises into the skies. The fierce glow in the blood lions' eyes. And the carefree way Killian laughs at it all. Human handlers chuckle as well. My heart sinks.

I've lost so much. My memories. My family. Gracie is all I have left.

I can not lose her too.

Spreading my wings, I take to the skies and target the blood lions. I must go swiftly. After all, my territory has limits. After twenty miles, my tail cuff won't allow me any farther. The blood lions have no such barriers, though. I simply must save Gracie before those demons get too far.

Before, the demons had a rhythm to their pacing. Now, I focus on the beat of their wings.

1, 2… 1, 2… 1, 2…

That rhythm is its own kind of music. Sure enough, the beat helps me access my magic. Power surges through my body, giving me extra speed. I use that velocity to close the distance between us. The smaller blood lion is my first quarry. I angle my head downward. A crown of horns encircles my temple. With an extra push of speed, I slam my head into the demon's side.

Thud!

My razor-sharp horns cut into the blood lion. It falters for a moment before spiraling toward the ground. The smaller demon then lands on the desert below with a whump and a geyser-like spray of sand. The little blood lion rests on its side, its spine arching at an odd angle. No question that the demon is dead.

That leaves the larger lion and Gracie.

The big demon still holds my tutor by her cloak. Gracie flails in its grip. Pushing myself with more power, I speed toward them both. I close the distance until the last demon flies right below me. Extending my legs, I rake my talons through its wings. The creature twitches, roars, and flaps with more fury.

Swooping down, I flip over onto my back. While flying upside-down, I speed beneath the blood lion, raking my back talons along its belly. With my front talons, I tear through the demon's throat.

The blood lion does as I hoped. It opens its mouth, releasing Gracie from its jaws. I gently scoop my tutor onto my front claws.

"Gracie?" I ask.

She doesn't reply.

Blood covers her everywhere. But is it because Gracie is injured... or did the blood come from my own talons and the other demons?

I speed to the ground. Half-way down, my body suddenly burns with pain. My right wing can no longer spread to its full width. Pain sears along my right side. I glance behind me.

Sure enough, my tail cuff glows bright red.

I've hit the barrier of my training grounds.

No, no, no.

The barrier acts as a wall, blocking my right wing while causing me pain. Still, I can use this magical barrier to save Gracie. Jutting out my hind legs, I kick against the invisible wall. Hurt radiates up my limbs. Even so, I get enough momentum to distance myself from the painful barrier. Diving down, I land onto the desert below and carefully set Gracie onto the sand.

"Gracie?" I ask.

No reply.

I quickly scan her body. My tutor is hurt. When the blood lion grabbed Gracie's cloak, it chewed into her back. All that blood I saw before? It was from Gracie. Now, she's passed out.

I force in a calming breath. Gracie is injured, not dead. I simply must summon healing magic before it's too late. Closing my eyes, I try to think of a rhythm. The beat is right there, like it was waiting for me. Words follow. There's something with hands and colors. I hold onto the tune.

A sense of electric power zooms through my veins. The air around Gracie turns hazy as if from too much heat. That's not warmth, however. It's my power.

Please, let it heal Gracie.

Slam!

Something wallops into my back. I'm thrown onto my side but hop back up to stand. Sure enough, my attacker is the larger blood dragon.

All the magic I'd summoned now pours through my limbs. White hot rage overtakes me. My thoughts become fragments. I am aware of my claws tearing. My jaws flip a body over. Next thing I know, the blood lion lies before me. It is in pieces. I take a half-step backward.

Did I do that?

No time to wonder. I must return to Gracie. Speeding over, I crouch by her side.

But I am too late. Tapping into my magic, I try to heal her. Magic swirls around me and into my friend. It is simply not enough. Gracie doesn't so much as twitch, let alone return to life. Perhaps if I could have accessed more of my powers, I might have been able to revive her. Yet I could not.

Gracie is dead.

Somehow I return to my cave, carrying Gracie in my claws. Killian has departed. My handlers remain and take Gracie away. At least, they've stopped laughing. I slump into my cave, where my handlers have left yet another pile of protein bars for me to eat. I poke at them with my talons.

I have no appetite anymore, either for food or to save myself before Friday. Perhaps it is time for things to end, once and for all.

RHODES, AGE NINETEEN

I hang out on the tour bus for Cool Daze, the worst *mindless sugar pop band* in the world. There are tons of things I'd rather be doing right now. Sleep, for one. Practicing battle moves is another. And let's not forget grabbing some dinner. That would be sweet. Yet I'm not doing any of that.

Nope.

Instead, I'm about to take a magical video call from Tempest and Portia, the Emperor and Empress of the Furor. My job? Explain to them why their daughter, Kaps, isn't here to talk to them personally.

This isn't the first time I've done this. It won't be the last. Doesn't make it suck any less, though.

The bus itself is empty. Nikki, our driver, is off at a hotel now while we finish tonight's gig. I scan the familiar space. Up front, the vehicle has these cushy seats. Typical bus stuff. But things don't stay regular here, considering how this place is for a band and all. In the bus' center, a row of cushy chairs face each other with a table between them. In the back, the chairs are gone, replaced by bunk beds with little curtains. This makes it easier to hit back-to-back gigs in different cities. That's what happens when your lead singer is both your manager and a dragon princess.

I sit at one of the center tables, waiting for the magical message to come through. Sure enough, a transparent version of the emperor and empress appear in the seats opposite me. Their images are slightly hazy.

"Do you accept our communication?" asks Portia. She won't see me until I give the okay.

"I accept."

A moment later, the transparent versions of Portia and Tempest come into clearer focus. Both are smiling. When they realize it's just me on the other side, their grins droop.

And here.

This moment.

It's why I hate doing these chats.

"Where is she?" asks Tempest. No question who *she* is in this question. *Kaps.*

"She went dancing last night with Chase." He's our lead guitar player and a wild card. Kaps can handle him, but still. "She knows to be here. I tried to find her but..." I shake my head. "I failed."

My insides churn with self-loathing. Here I am, supposedly her personal guard. Yet I can't keep track of her half the time. Sure, her sister Huntress also trails Kaps secretly—it's easier to do when you're a glass dragon and can turn invisible—but even so. It's my job and I'm failing at it.

"We've spoken to Huntress," says Tempest. "Kaps is fine. Don't worry, mate." Somewhere along the line, I got to be on a first name basis with Tempest and Portia. It's weird.

"Evidently, there is a great dance club nearby," adds Portia.

I rub my temples. "Maybe we should call Atlas back." We have this *how about Atlas* conversation a lot. My uncle Atlas is also a trained guard, same as I am. The big difference? He doesn't put up with anything.

"Kaps can't stand him," says Portia. "When Atlas is around, Kaps runs off and hides so well, even Huntress can't find her."

I sigh. "We could always lock Kaps in the tower." I'm even half-serious. The place is like a resort on lock-down.

A long pause follows. Tempest and Portia share a long look.

My eyes widen. "That was a joke."

"We've given Kaps a lot of freedom," says Portia. "There's no question why she's so reckless."

The words hang out there, unspoken and painful. Kaps went unhinged after Zin died. Bands of sorrow tighten around my throat. I picture the little pixie in a red dress who made up words for *Our Song*. That was a lifetime ago.

"Yet we can't let this go on forever," says Tempest.

"Kaps is on her last chance," adds Portia. "She must return to the palace in time for the ceremony celebrating the high point of Pandora's starfall. That's her eighteenth birthday as well."

I nod. "Kaps knows about that. She's on board. I'll make it happen."

"You can't make Kaps do anything," says Tempest. "You've got to prepare yourself, mate."

I tilt my head. "Prepare?"

"For your life after being Kaps' guard," answers Portia. "Once she's secure, you're too talented to sit outside her door forever. Tempest and I have some ideas."

I lean back in the chair. My mind blanks with shock. *They can't mean this.*

All of a sudden, the front doors of the bus open with a squeal. Our drummer, Bash, walks up the short flight of steps. He's a young and bald dude with a square face and chocolate-colored skin. He is also the only *sane* member of the band. Which is odd, considering how Bash is the drummer.

"Hey," says Bash. "We've got sound trouble."

I refocus on Portia and Tempest. "I've got to run. We're

playing a big festival tonight. Seems like I need to check some stuff."

"Think on your future," says Tempest.

"And have a great show," adds Portia.

The images of the emperor and empress flare more brightly for a moment. After that, they vanish. Tempest's words echo through my heart.

Think on your future.

Is there a life for me after being Kaps' guard? I honestly don't know.

RHODES

*A*fter stepping off the bus, I'm hit with a wave of scorching air. I'm a water dragon, so having a festival gig in the desert? *Ouch.* The fact that the show is called Trance-a-dance? *Also painful.*

Bash and I march through the crowd. It's mostly humans here. There are a few Furor (not that mortals can tell the difference.) Many dragon shifters escaped to Earth when Chimera took over. Even though Portia and Tempest are great rulers, Chimera was still around for a long time. As a result, we now have a big ex-pat population on Earth.

"You owe me another one," says Bash.

I bob my head, thinking about all the times Bash has interrupted with a so-called *emergency* to get me out of chatting with the imperial parents. "How many favors are we up to?"

Bash chuckles. "At least seven hundred. I plan to be repaid one day. Handsomely."

"Bad planning there, bub. I'm a grunt who tracks the princess. Not a lot of upward mobility to pay back favors."

"We'll see."

We reach a line of tall metal fences with the name Trance-a-dance written on a sign above. Beyond those metal barriers stands the main stage. This is the full festival deal with crazy-tall monitors and a custom light show. It's for the big players, though. We're a warm up band. Basically, we play on one of the small stages that are set apart from the main drag.

For us, this is a still big gig, however. No doubt, Kaps pulled some magical strings to get us in. As a manager, she's good that way ... except when she isn't.

At last, Bash and I reach a tiny stage. The audience area is marked by fabric walls. They look like sheets on poles. A small sound board sits on a table in back. I scan the space and groan.

"I'd say there's a sound problem," I announce. "There's an *everything problem.*"

The stage is empty. No mics. Our equipment isn't even here, let alone set up. As manager, Kaps is supposed to make sure this stuff is in place. But that's Cool Daze for you. We're a hot mess.

It's a good thing I got here in time. "Thanks, Bash."

"You want help?" asks our drummer.

"No, I owe you enough favors already. I'll get the equipment in, just make sure the band takes it the last mile." In other words, I'm not tuning Chase's guitar.

"Will do." Bash saunters off into the crowd.

It takes some running around, but I find the festival logistics crew, discover where our equipment went, and get it hauled over to the mini stage for tonight's show. Some guys come by and say they're the extra security. I checked out their bios before—all of them seem legit. Doesn't hurt to have extra hands around, so I give them a big welcome.

Once the stage is somewhat set-up, I head back to our prep tent. Outside, it's another white structure like all the other stuff at Trance-a-dance. Inside, there's a water cooler and a bunch of bean bags. As dressing rooms go, I've seen worse.

I find Kaps laying on a line of bags, looking through her data pad. No doubt, she's on the trail of another *magical something.*

Today she's wearing a new enchanted wig. This time, it's pink mohawk. She has hundreds of these, I swear.

As for the rest of the band, Bash sits in a corner, playing with his smart phone. Livingston, our bass player, paces the space. He's a wiry guy with big knees and a concave chest. As always, he wears a mask.

Yes, I said mask. And today's variety is a white lamb.

The whole thing isn't as odd as it sounds. Cool Daze sometimes puts on masks during performances. Livingston's the only one who leaves them on 24-7. He's a strange ranger, but it's not like there are ton of volunteers who'll leave Furonium and hang out with the crazy princess. If I hadn't vowed to keep her safe, I'd have run off long ago.

Kaps glances up from her data pad. "Hey, Rhodes."

She's totally oblivious. *That ticks me off.* "Your parents say hello."

"That's nice."

I ball my hands into fists. "I'm here to guard you, not make excuses to the emperor and empress."

"But you did anyway." Kaps sighs. "You're the best, Rhodes. I don't know what I'd do without you." For a moment, she's there. Zin's twin sister, raw and in pain.

What would I do if I weren't her guard?

"Has Huntress been watching you?" I ask.

"Who knows? These days she splits her time between me and L'Griffe."

Which makes sense. Huntress has good reason to get to know L'Griffe. After all, Kaps has been ticking them off for ages. Huntress needs to be prepared for retaliation.

Livingston stops pacing. "This is a serious show," he says. "People live in this corner of the desert for days, staking out a place. We're not ready." He points to Kaps. "You need to do something called *rehearse.*"

Kaps doesn't look up from her data pad. "Chase and I

are fine."

For the first time, I notice Chase laying face-down on a pile of bean bags. Our lead guitar player looks passed out.

"I'm concerned," states Livingston. "If we don't take this seriously, then our audience won't either."

"Then lose the lambie," says Bash. That's a lot of advice from our drummer, by the way. Normally, he says zero in group settings.

Livingston fidgets with his mask. "This is my signature in the band. Masks, man. It's very important to have a brand." He then spends a few minutes talking about rehearsal schedules. Then bunk assignments. Livingston is a chatterbox. I pay attention more than most, and I'm barely listening. There's no point interrupting, either. The guy will just blab until he's done.

"You don't need a signature," says Kaps at last. "You're not the lead singer."

Livingston still wears his mask and paces the floor. For a bass player, the guy is borderline hyperactive. "All the more reason for *you* not to be terrible at your job," he snaps. "Rehearse."

Kaps shrugs. "It's on the list."

I walk over to Chase, not because I want his opinion, but to see if the guy is okay. Normally, Chase loves these 'stop sucking' fights. I pause beside him. "Chase, what do you say?" I ask. "Should we push off our start time? Livingston may have a point." At that last comment, Livingston launches into another monologue about how he always has the best insights of everyone.

Yet, there's no response from Chase.

Kneeling down, I shake the guy's shoulder. "Hey, man. You okay?" There's a loud snore in my face, followed by the reek of alcohol. The scent is so strong, I'm surprised my eyebrows aren't signed off.

I turn to Kaps. "Why is our lead guitarist passed out?"

Livingston pipes up. "They went dancing last night."

"And this morning," adds Bash.

"I get that." I look to Kaps. "You don't drink."

"Duh." Kaps rolls her eyes. "Can I help it if Chase does? He's a million years old."

At this, Chase lifts his head. "I'm twenty-two."

I widen my eyes in mock surprise. "He speaks."

Kaps sits upright. "Oh wow! I'm a *wanted woman* at last!" She reads from her tablet. "Offered: one case of rubies for the Furor who finds Kappa Psi Phi Sigma, also known as Kaps, also known as the lead singer for Cool Daze. And it's posted by actual agents of L'Griffe." She pumps her fist. "Best one yet."

"Nice work, Kaps." That's Livingston. Sometimes, that dude can be such a kiss ass. "What did you steal from them this time?"

"A tail cuff. It was an ancient model with magic and runes. L'Griffe got it back, but it was mine for seventeen minutes."

"Is that what you were *really* doing last night?" I ask.

"Of course," says Kaps. "Dancing with Chase was the perfect cover. I got the cuff, they got the cuff. It was a blast."

"How do things work with you and L'Griffe, exactly?" asks Livingston.

"You already know," I grumble.

But Kaps loves telling this story. Now that Livingston has opened the topic, she's all in.

"It's like this," begins Kaps. "L'Griffe and I have similar interests in dragon artifacts. They locate them, I steal them, and then they sneak them back. Every once in a while, they put out a bounty on my head. No one is dumb enough to go after Princess Kaps, though. It's all in good fun."

"Adrenaline junkie," says Bash.

Kaps rolls her eyes. "What's wrong with that?"

I pinch the bridge of my nose. "I should drag your ass back to Furonium now."

"You should," says Kaps. "But you won't."

"Watch it," I warn. "One day, you'll push me too far."

"But you won't let me do that," says Kaps. "Come on. They've tried every warrior in Furonium as my guard. You're the best there is when it comes to managing me. If you won't guard me, what's left?"

I level her with a serious look. "The tower, Kaps."

She pauses and considers this. For a second, I hope that I've finally broken through to the princess. Will she stop being stuck at eight years old and actually grow up?

Kaps saunters over. "Good thing you'll always guard me, then." She air kisses my cheek. After that, the princess steps over to Chase and kicks his ankle. "Wake up, already." She leans in and sniffs. "Whoa. Not good." Kaps focuses on me once more. "When are we on again?"

There's a moment where I debate continuing the tower conversation, but there really isn't time... or a point to trying to force Kaps into anything.

"We start in twenty minutes." I fold my arms over my chest. "We're in the first round of warm-up acts, so maybe we could switch with someone later. If we need more time, we might be able to get it."

"Nah." Kaps shrugs. "We'll all wear our ghost masks." She points at my nose. "And *you'll* play lead guitar."

Kaps does this every so often. Most of the time, I make her rally Chase. My guitar days are over.

"Ghost masks!" cries Livingston. "Sweet! This lamb one is starting to smell inside."

"Try using a toothbrush," deadpans Bash.

Kaps winks in my direction. "Better warm up your fingers, Rhodes. You're on in twenty." She blows me another kiss. Kaps treats me like every other guy she flirts with. Only we've never so much as kissed. I hook up with human groupies and then only rarely. Things with Kaps are complex enough as it is.

Bash steps up to my side. "You up for this?" he asks. Bash is a great drummer, and he gets how I love to play.

The idea rattles around my soul. *Music*. Sometimes, it still does call to me. When that happens, I play enough to scratch the itch, then get back to work.

"Well." I rub my chin, considering. "It could work. The rave has hired its own muscle. They'll be good enough for tonight." I round on our lead singer. "And this is an exception, not the rule."

Kaps grins. "You're the best."

Livingston opens a box, yanks out a mask, and hands it to me. I shake my head. "And I'm not wearing a stupid ghost mask. It's already a million degrees out there."

"But that breaks our band's look," whines Livingston. "You should wear the mask or revive Chase."

Kaps steps over. "I could cast a few resuscitation spells." She grips his bangs, which are exceptionally long. In one smooth move, Kaps yanks Chase's face up from the bean bags. "Are you in there?"

"My name is Chase and I run after the princess."

At least, that's logical and true. Chase has been hitting on Kaps for months. She sees him as anything but dating material.

"Maybe we can sober the guy up," says Livingston.

Chase's eyes go wide. "Mambo the tiger!" A long burp follows. "Skinny my fighter jet!" Then he face-plants back onto the beanbag.

Kaps lets out a low whistle. "What the hell was that?"

"Bad news," declares Bash.

"Right," says Kaps. "I could cast some spells to sober Chase up, but the way he looks now? Healing him could take hours." Kaps rounds on me. "Fine. You don't have to wear the stupid mask."

Livingston frowns. "It still ruins the band's look."

"No one notices Chase anyway," says Bash. "All eyes are on the royal here." Which is a positive soliloquy from our drummer.

"Damned right, it's all about me." Kaps swaps out her pink mohawk for a wig with purple curls. "Let's go make some music."

And so, we're off.

5

ZINNIA

I stare at my pile protein bars and wait for the last of my handlers to leave. When I'm this miserable, only one thing makes me feel better.

It seems to take forever, but eventually my handlers depart. Once they are all gone, I take to my human form and visit a particular spot in my home cave. There, in a far off nook, I dig through the sand and uncover my most important treasure: a small book. It shows pictures of ladies with tall white hair and strange dresses. Some ride in wagons with horses. There are also preprinted words on the pages. I can still read them. The cover reads, *A Child's Primer For Music.*

With my pointer finger, I trace the letters C… H… I… L… D.

I flip through the pages, finding some insect-like markings. These squiggly lines are important, but I don't remember why, exactly. There are also hand-written words at the end of the book, but whenever I try to read them, I see that awful crystal ball in my mind. The mother of all headaches follows. Sometimes I don't sleep for days afterwards. As a result, I limit my book time to tracing letters and looking at the pictures. That always cheers me up.

Suddenly, I hear the roar of human voices. These aren't my handlers, though. I step outside my cave once more. The sun touches the horizon. Winds have changed. Fresh scents carry on the air. Hundreds of humans are near.

No, thousands.

I follow the the scent to the edge of my territory. As I reach the magical boundary, the cuff on my tail glows red. I can't go farther.

That's when I hear it — a sound that shatters my world.

Music.

The knowledge hits me with a wallop. That's what those little insect-like markings were about. *Music.* Nothing is more important to me. Or perhaps that is how things were in the past.

I kneel down in the sand and listen to a sound I'd forgotten even existed. For a sweet moment, I feel whole once more.

6

RHODES

I stand on stage, holding Chase's guitar. What a piece of crap. It's covered in a thin layer of slime from *who knows what*. A real musician takes care of their instrument.

Then again, none of us are real musicians.

The large white sheets that mark our area flap a little in the breeze. A handful of humans mill about the right side of the dance pit. I can't help but notice that's where the shade is. They don't look ready to hear music so much as to avoid rays from the setting sun.

In a corner, the human sound team glares at us. We didn't do a sound check. Now, we're milling about the stage without any idea when we'll start. We're never getting invited back here again.

Beside me, Kaps fiddles with her guitar for a bit, then pulls the microphone closer. "Let's hear it for Cool Daze!"

The handful of sun-avoiders don't even flinch, let alone cheer or anything. So humiliating.

"Our first tune goes out to L'Griffe, who think they'll get the next item on my list, which is none other than Pandora's box. But I'll find it first, right?"

Again, no response.

Now, these are clueless humans. No one's taking notes on dragon mafioso groups. But this is L'Griffe. Kaps can't go around taunting them. They're murderers and exiles from Furonium. Every emperor and empress tries to wipe them out; all of them fail, including Tempest and Portia.

"One, two," says Kaps. "One, two, three go!"

No one goes.

Kaps looks around. "Come on, guys. Back me up."

"You refused to do a set list," I say. "Unless we've got a new counting song, no one knows what you want."

Kaps narrows her eyes at me. She hates being corrected on stage. Well, I hate the fact that my life is tied to hers, so we're even.

"Fine," says Kaps. "Lets play *Dance It.*" She starts into the opening riff. Kaps could be a decent guitar player, but she doesn't so much strum the instrument as punish it. And she also makes stuff up on the fly, let's not forget. It's why we need both a bass and lead guitarist. It smoothes out the sound.

Kaps finishes the riff and grabs the microphone. If there's a benefit to this song, it's that Kaps doesn't have much of a guitar solo here. She starts howling out the words.

> *Me and my crew*
> *We dance, dance, dance*
> *Guys eye me up*
> *Don't stand a chance, chance, chance*

I play out Chase's part and mentally plan how I'll get in touch with Huntress. Kaps now has a bounty on her head from L'Griffe. And she's trying to steal more stuff they want, namely Pandora's box. That can't be good.

The song ends. Kaps rounds on me.

"Since you pointed out we don't have a set, why don't you pick the next song?" she asks.

"I'll pass."

"Pick the tune, sweetie." There's nothing sweet in her tone though.

And in that moment, I snap. It's all too much: covering up for Kaps to my emperor and empress… following her around to random gigs with two fans who aren't even fans… and the fact that she doesn't respect music. It's more like sees it as a dodge to do what she *really* wants, which is to get into a war with a mafioso outfit that steals Furor relics.

And this is my life. Hey, I get it. I made my vow. Doesn't mean I have to every little thing that Kaps wants.

On reflex, I play the opening chords to *Our Song*. None of the other guys step in. They've never heard this tune before. Beside me, Kaps frowns. "Not that, Rhodes. Stop."

Still, I keep going. The music takes me to a dreamlike place. In my heart, I'm back with Zin. I picture the words in my mind.

> *Gray or green or brown or yellow*
> *Your look could change just like the rainbow*

A roar sounds from across the desert. Whatever. My fingers have started to play on their own. I've lost everything. My music. Zin. My pride. I'm finishing the tune.

> *I wouldn't care*
> *It's what we share*
> *You're mine*

Warmth spread through my heart. Memories of Zin return: The way her cherub face brightened when she smiled … How I only felt complete when we were together … And every time she wrote the words while I made the tune.

Oh, my sweet lost rhana.

7

ZINNIA

*T*he desert looks pretty this time of day. Red shadows play across the sand. For a time, I stand still and listen to the music. Somehow I know it's not fine music, but I treasure it just the same.

A new song wafts across the air. Every cell in my human-shaped body goes on alert. This tune familiar somehow. That crystal ball appears in my mind. Faces flash within its depths.

I know this song. It's from my past.

My temples throb with pain, but I hold onto that crystal ball image. The round orb stays hazy and then—*whoa*—a clear image appears. It's a tail. Only it's not mine or Killian's. Nope. This tail is covered in green scales.

It's another Furor. Did a dragon shifter like me write this song?

Invisible tethers of memory pull me forward, urging me to march past the barrier. That song is important. The person who wrote it? Even more so. A fluttery sensation spreads across my rib cage. It's been a long time since I've felt anything other than rage or boredom, I have a hard time placing the emotion. It might be affection. Or it could even be something with a magic all its own.

And that's when it happens.

Snap.

My tail cuff cracks. Where once it was a smooth loop of red stone, now there's a long fissure along the surface. Not enough to make it come off, but it could be enough of a break to cause something else.

Could I leave my grounds?

Is that even possible?

Taking in a deep breath, I reach forward. There's no missing the moment when I cross over the invisible barrier that separates my lands from the rest of the human world. Pain encircles my fingertips and shoots around my palm. Soon my entire arm feels like it is on fire.

But my hand is past the barrier. That's never happened before.

The music echoes across the desert, more beautiful than before. Every corner of my soul wants to pass the barrier and discover the secret of that tune. Before, I might have worried what would happen to Gracie if I left. Sadly, that's no longer a concern.

I inch closer to the barrier.

My thoughts race through every reason why leaving is a terrible idea. I could die crossing this invisible wall. And even if I do escape, my handlers will come after me. Sure, they are human, but they also trained me. They know my every move before I make it. And let's not forget my vow. I promised to become the Vessel of the Future in six days. And there's my family to consider. What if Killian is telling the truth? I may really be the the last Furor and the only way to raise my people.

I can't leave here.

More of the tune reverberates across the desert. As the notes move through me, another argument appears. If I am really dying in six days, then shouldn't I live the rest of my life to its fullest? And if the humans come after me, it may absolutely be another fight, but couldn't that be worth it? Plus, if I do keep my vow, I want to know if Killian has been speaking the truth. Am I truly the last of my kind?

Time to find out.

Straightening my spine, I step across the barrier. Pain burns across my human form, but it quickly fades. And the music still calls to me.

I take off across the sands.

8

ZINNIA

Once I cross the barrier, I become aware of the scorching heat on my human form. Not sure if the excitement of the music was blocking it before—or if there was some kind of protection from hurt within my home boundary. Yet whatever the reason, the dying sunlight now burns my skin. Hot sand sears the soles of my bare feet. A question arises. Do I shift into my dragon form? I can certainly cross the desert more quickly that way.

No.

For some reason, the very thought of turning into a full dragon brings a foul taste to my mouth. It was Killian who always urged me to stay in Furor form. For now, I wish to stay human. That said, I don't wish to fry in the sun, either. So I change shape until I am half-way between a human and a dragon. My skin becomes covered in gray scales, including my feet. It is far more pleasant.

With my new appearance in place, I march across the desert. With each step, the music grows louder. Soon the beat thrums through my chest. Scents fill the air. Perfume. Sweat. The smell of food cooking. My mouth waters at the thought. Not sure how I know there are better things to dine upon than protein bars, but there is no doubt about it. If I can find a meal here, I will take it.

The music becomes louder and different. More than one band plays now. Perhaps many were always many groups, but for some reason I only heard one before. I set aside the thought for later.

In no time, I come upon a patchwork of small white tents before a sea of larger white structures. These tiny tents must be outliers from the rest of the human dwellings. Every so often, a wooden sign sticks up from the sand, saying *toilets*, *buses*, or *food* along with an arrow symbol. *Interesting.*

A human woman sits before one of the tents. Twisting around, the woman's head is half-way through the tent's entrance flap. A pang of longing moves through my torso. I can't remember seeing another face besides Gracie's and Killian's. My other handlers all wear masks. What will this mortal look like? A white blanket is spread out before her on the sand. Upon that surface are stacked different body coverings. The sign reads *Trance-a-dance T-shirts*. I pause before the display and wait.

"I told you, we should move closer to the stage," she says to someone within the tent. "No one's out here."

"Then we should have gotten a permit like everyone else," replies a man's voice. "This is the best we can do."

While the two talk, I look down at my scaled skin. Humans can't see my scales or tail. To mortals, I simply appear naked. I remember the pictures of humans in my little book. All the women wore fancy dresses. If I'm to discover where *my music* came from, I must blend in.

My music.

Those two words rattle around my mind. Why would I think some random tune was mine? Instantly the crystal ball appears in my mind's eye. This time, it doesn't spin with hazy images. Instead, random strains of music waft from its center. *Odd.*

Shaking my head, I refocus on the moment. I don't want to miss my first encounter with someone who's not Killian or

Gracie. While I wait, I scoop up the largest shirt I can find and slip it over my body. It easily comes down to my knees. Perfect. I look like a regular human now. To complete the look, I even transform from scales back to regular skin.

At last, the woman turns around. She has overlarge eyes, a small chin and a haggard look on her face. A worry demon gnaws on her ear. This is a tiny, frog-like creature with pointed teeth. Again, it is invisible to humans. But the little monster sends a steady stream of anxiety into this mortal's soul. Such a shame.

The woman turns to me and beams. She even has little crinkle lines by her eyes and mouth. "Sorry, didn't see you here." She eyes my shirt. "I take it you're buying that?"

I tilt my head. "Buying?" Things just are offered to me. It's always been that way. Somehow, I know it was that way even before I lost my memory.

"Yes." The woman holds out her hand. "We take cash here."

Now this part makes some sense. My handlers don't talk to me, but sometimes they chat with each other. I've overheard them complaining about needing more cash to get things. This must be what they meant.

"I carry no human money."

The woman shakes her head. "First customer we get all day and she can't pay."

My eyes widen as an idea forms. "I can help you with your worry demon."

The woman winces as if a foul smell just hit her. "Worry demon?"

"The one on your ear. It makes you anxious, does it not?"

"I don't know what you're talking about." Even so, she says the words without any conviction.

Which makes sense. Humans can't see demons, but they do sense them on some level.

"How about this?" I offer. "I take the demon away, and if you feel better, then we shall consider my debt paid."

The woman grins. "I've been doing this for years. Been offered all sorts of stuff in barter. But you're the first one with demon removal." She throws up her hands. "All right. Do your thing."

Stepping forward, I order my tail into action. It spears the demon and pulls it away from its unwilling host. Instantly the woman exhales.

"That's it?" she asks.

"Yes, it is done."

She gives me a wary glance. "If you say so."

Pausing, I consider this turn of events. When Killian does things, it always includes some kind of ceremony. Perhaps this human expects one as well. I raise my arms. "And with the power I wield as the Vessel of the Future, I hereby present you with a dead anxiety demon." My tail does its part by arching over my shoulder and displaying the skewered frog demon. "Now you are free, free, FREE!" As I say the word *free* for the last time, I even force my eyes to light up with demonic power. Maybe that will help on some level.

The woman sets her hand on her throat. "I do feel better."

"You are most welcome," I say.

With my work done, I head off in the direction of the music once more.

9

ZINNIA

I walk away from the vendor and head toward the scent of humans and food. As I move forward, the tents grow so numerous, it becomes a challenge to step around them. The music grows louder as well. More bands play on top of each other, creating a mishmash of sound that makes my head hurt. I'm no longer following a single tune. Instead, the crush of the crowd merely pushes me forward.

Was it only a few minutes ago I saw my first face since Killian? Now, there are so many humans around, it overloads my senses. There's a young boy in a pointed hat. A group of humans dressed as clowns. A pair of mortals pressing their mouths together in a kiss. I glimpse others rolling around inside their tents, their bodies moving together. My handlers do such things. I don't understand the appeal.

Soon, it becomes too much. My ears ring. Spots of white cloud my vision. I hug my elbows while I stumble along. One fact becomes clear. This was a mistake. I wanted to leave my home in order to explore the world for a few days. This was supposed to be fun. It is not. Perhaps I should change into dragon form and fly away.

A scent reaches me. The hint of moonlight and spices. Furor are near.

Wait, Furor?

No wonder the music called to me. Furor may be playing music nearby. Perhaps the first tune I heard was part of my blood or history.

A voice blares over the desert. "Welcome to Trance-a-dance. Check out our virtual club spaces for local bands. The big show starts on the main stage at 10 PM."

All my focus locks onto that scent. Furor. I follow it into a small place marked with large sheets. Unlike the rest of the place, this area is fairly deserted. There are more people on stage than listening in the crowd. But the ones who are playing?

My world stops.

They are Furor.

10

RHODES

*T*here's no set list, so we just keep playing whatever strikes Kaps as fun. Bash goes nuts on drums. Livingston strums out a bass line on his guitar. He's loving his new mask, by the way. How do I know? Livingston keeps dancing while playing. He isn't the greatest dancer—he's all stiff except for his hips, which he swivels around in a great circle. That said, who am I to judge? The guy is happy. A new mask does that for him.

Kaps grabs the microphone once more. "This is a love song. It's called, *Me Me Me.*"

I fight the urge to roll my eyes. Only Kaps would think a love song would have that particular name. Last time I checked, love was supposed to be a mutual thing where you spend at least some time thinking about the other person.

Without any more lead in, Kaps jumps right into the opening guitar riff. She must have boosted her amp, because the speakers squeal with feedback. The humans working the sound table hate this, by the way. She didn't give a beat countdown or anything, so there's no time to check levels. One of the mortals flips us the finger while Kaps jumps right into the lyrics.

Fight for me
Live for me
Break your back
Die for me
It's all about me
Me, me, me
Me, me, me
Me, me, me, me, me, ME, me!

This tune is another yell-fest. I can play lead guitar for it in my sleep. Which is a good thing. Sure, we have extra help, but my real job here is still to keep an eye on the crowd and threats. Yet for some reason, my attention can't stay anywhere today. Nervous energy twists through my limbs. It's like I'm five years old again and waiting to open my first birthday present.

I force my training through my mind. There's a regular circuit of stuff I need to track: entrances, exits, and most important of all, potential targets. Four humans still lurk in the shade. A pair of security guards hang by the sound mixing board. An older Furor hobbles to the tent to stand in the sunshine. Orange scales. Those kind love heat. No threat there.

A new face becomes clear from the far corner. A girl Furor. She looks fit and lean in her bulky T-shirt. White dreads hang to her shoulders. My breath catches. I even forget where I am in the song. My entire body falls still. Kaps starts playing my line to make up for it—something that never happens—and shoots me a warning glance.

I nod and pick up the tune where I left off. Still, my attention stays locked on the girl. Something about her calls to me. The beautiful line of her cheek. How strength seems to pulse through her limbs. The way intelligence dances in her bright blue eyes. It's hypnotic.

And strange.

This isn't me. I don't respond this way, even to Furor girls.

My focus is always on one thing—keeping Kaps safe. Not even music is more important. It's been that way since Zin died.

And now, here's a random Furor Girl at this abandoned corner of the worst desert festival ever. And she has my attention drawn in like nothing else before.

My military training knows what this is.

Trouble.

11

ZINNIA

I stare and stare. This can't be right. There's a girl here with purple hair. Men who play drums and guitar. All of them have tails.

A chill rolls up my spine, despite the heat.

My handlers lied to me.

I am not the last of my kind.

Rage tightens every muscle in my body. In my fury, I barely notice the bomb sitting atop what humans call the stage.

But it is there.

A long braid of yellow and orange wires stick out from the side of a tall black box that blares out sounds. The words *speaker 2* are painted along its side.

I shake my head. Gracie taught me all about bombs with braided wires. Certain warriors build their devices this way. Deadly. At a minimum, this kind of weapon would kill everyone within a quarter mile.

Not good.

If this were a battle, I'd simply toss the bomb at my enemy. I've practiced that scenario with my handlers many times. Yet there is no one here I wish to kill. And I could throw the bomb away, but not far enough to save the humans.

Fear rattles me to the bone. What can I do?

As if my a magnetic pull, I stare at one of the Furor men playing guitar. He has a green tail, solid build and bright eyes. A warrior's look. I feel certain of one thing.

If anyone can stop that bomb, it is that dragon man.

RHODES

I'm only vaguely aware of the band. Our music. Even my job as guard. Instead, my focus stays locked on Furor Girl. Every line of her body freezes.

Is she all right?

As if she can hear me, her gaze meets mine. An invisible tether reaches out from her soul. There's a line of connection between us that I could never have imagined. This isn't something that just formed. Somehow, it already exists.

But that can't be right. All the drama of Kaps and Cool Daze must be getting to me.

Still, I sense emotions through our joined consciousness.

The chill of alarm.

A weight of fear.

The electric charge of desperation for me to do something.

I strum my cords without thinking about them. There's a definite connection here; I'm not imagining this. Furor Girl wants—no, needs—me to take some action. She stares in a particular direction. Every line of her body seems to scream, *this is it!*

I follow her line of vision and gasp.

There's a bomb in one of the speakers.

Instinct takes over. I drop Chase's guitar and race for the speaker. All the while, I pull on every internal shred of Electrophus magic within me. Power charges inside my muscles. Then it pops over my skin, creating a webwork of thin lines of lighting.

I raise my arms with my palms flat and forward. All the years of training from Father echo through my mind.

Grab the magic.

Focus it.

Release.

So that's what I do. Gathering my power, I press it toward the speaker. Webs of lightning shoot off my hands, creating a cage around the speaker. This is something the humans will see. It's unavoidable.

Boom!

The speaker explodes. Plumes of fire tear up from the device and combine with my cage-work of lighting. A column of light stretches into the sky, blinding in its brightness. Shredded metal and plastic burst out toward the crowd. I focus my lightning, burning those pieces to ash.

A thought strikes me. My lighting is what took Father's funeral barge away. Now it erases this bomb.

Good.

Our small audience gasps and claps at the sight. They think this is all part of the show.

Even better.

Bits of shrapnel flare more brightly as they slam against the blast radius of my lightning orb. Seconds tick away as the pillar of fire and lightning dies down. My powers burn through the shattered speaker.

Soon the flames die out altogether. I rise and wave to the handful of folks in the crowd. Bash launches into an impromptu drum solo. One person cheers. The security guys do not look happy, though. They march to the front of our small stage.

"What the hell was that?" asks one. He's got a square face and no neck.

"Laser light show," I reply. "Crowd loved it."

"You need to get that approved first," snarls the guard. Raising his voice, he addresses the rest of the band. "Off the stage. Now!"

Kaps shrugs. "Fine with me."

As Cool Daze marches away, I scan the crowd for Furor Girl, the one who warned me about the bomb.

She's gone.

Before I have time to process that little tragedy, I notice someone else is here. Someone with violet eyes, brown hair, and battle leathers. I catch the barest glimpse of her before she vanishes.

Huntress.

Kaps' sister has a gift for knowing when a certain princess is in trouble. Which is a good thing. Keeping Kaps alive is a team sport.

As I step offstage, I spy something gleaming on the sand. *Metal.* Kneeling down, I scoop the item from the ground. A small piece of the bomb survived my lightning. My breath catches. The image of a dragon's claw is painted on the metal surface.

That's the symbol of L'Griffe.

RHODES

The minute we're all inside the tent, everyone returns to their usual spots. Bash takes his seat. Livingston resumes his nervous pacing. Chase remains face-planted into a bean bag. Kaps lounges and checks her data pad. That won't last long. I've got lots to discuss with the princess.

"That was a disaster," I state.

"I know, right?" Kaps rounds on me. "What was that about? You can't go setting up laser light shows without telling anyone."

I grip the charred metal in my fist. "That wasn't part of the show. It was a bomb. From L'Griffe."

Kaps pales. "How do you know?"

I hold up the scrap for everyone to see. "It has the L'Griffe emblem on the side. I put the rest together. I'm smart that way."

"Whatever," says Kaps. "It's the thing the audience liked the most, so I guess it's fine." She tears off her purple wig. "Besides, L'Griffe never gets close enough to cause trouble."

I can't believe this. "They just did, Kaps."

She points to her face. "Not worried. I have you."

I lower my voice. "I am not perfect."

"Damn right, you're not. What was that all about on stage? *Our Song*, really? You know what that tune does to me."

This is a very Kaps thing to do, by the way. She's a master of changing the subject when she doesn't want to face something. In this case, Kaps wants to avoid the fact that L'Griffe is getting too close. I open my mouth, ready to launch into a speech about the insanity of bringing up *Our Song*.

That's when she steps in.

Furor Girl.

Up close, she's even more magnetic. She has a wide mouth. Long limbs. An air of energy about her. A weight I hadn't known I carried now seeps from my shoulders.

Kaps eyes the new girl from head to toe. Twice. "She's ..." Kaps bobs her head while she searches for the right word.

My instincts tell me this is important. *What does Kaps make of this stranger?* I step closer.

"She's what?" I ask.

"Creepy," finishes Kaps.

I take a pointed step away from the princess. "False." Not sure why, but I feel very protective of Furor Girl.

Livingston adjusts his mask. It's a move he does so the eye-holes better match with his vision. He's checking out Furor Girl as well.

"She's Thorntail," says Livingston. "And a scrub."

"Don't say scrub," warns Bash. His tail arches up, showing off the multi-colored pattern along the bottom. The implication is clear: *I'm a scrub, too. Watch it.*

"Whoa, so sensitive," says Livingston.

Bash doesn't back down. "Damned right."

Livingston raises his hands in the universal move for, *fine I'm out of here.* "This is me, leaving for the bus."

"Bus is locked until your gear is packed," I warn.

"Who says?" asks Livingston.

"Me," I reply. "I've got the keys. Pack up your crap and we'll meet at the buses later. I am not moving your junk around again, especially after I almost got blown up for you guys." I look to Kaps. "Any problems?"

"Nope." Kaps says the word absently. Her mind is somewhere else for sure. "That's totally cool." The princess steps towards Furor Girl. No question what's captured Kaps' interest. Furor Girl wears a tail cuff.

I huff out a long breath. *Kaps and her love of bright, shiny objects.*

Kaps shoots Furor Girl a brilliant smile. "You know what?"

Furor Girl tilts her head. She's curious, but doesn't answer. *Smart.*

"That tail cuff you're wearing?" asks Kaps. "That looks just like something I stole from L'Griffe. Only the one I took was white." She steps closer. "Can I hold it for a second?"

Furor Girl growls. Kaps freezes in place.

I don't bother hiding my smile. *That was awesome, right there.* No one stops Kaps from doing anything.

Kaps pauses for a moment, then giggles. "Fine. You can keep it."

I take another step closer to Furor Girl. "Why are you here?" I ask her.

Furor Girl starts to sing.

> *Me and my crew*
> *We dance, dance, dance*
> *Guys eye me up*
> *Don't stand a chance, chance, chance*

She says it slower, like a musical chant instead of how Kaps does it. Furor Girl's voice even has a little rasp to it. I can't help it; the way she sings the tune changes the music for me. What if we played that song more slowly? We could even give it more of a Spanish acoustic feel. Fresh guitar riffs echo through my head.

"She knows our lyrics." Livingston beams. "That makes her a fan."

Furor Girl nods. "I liked your music." She points to me. "Mostly his." Can't help it. A sense of pride warms my chest.

She likes my music.

Kaps sniffs. "Rude."

"Glad you like my music." I inch even closer to Furor Girl. Every cell in my body wants me to brush against her skin. I don't, though. Furor Girl strikes me as the skittish type. "And thanks for pointing out the bomb."

"I knew you would fix it." Furor Girl pins me with her gaze. She's got one of those honest and open looks that just tears you wide open.

"It goes with the job," I explain.

"You are Furor," she says in her raspy voice.

"Yeah." I gesture around the room. "All of us are."

"So I'm not the only one." That open look of hers turns shuttered. Cold. Something is wrong. Bands of sadness tighten about my throat.

"No, you're not alone." I don't know why I say that. It just feels natural.

Furor Girl's big blue eyes lock with my gaze. It's as if the rest of the tent vanishes, including the other folks in the band. There's no Bash in the corner, playing drums on his thighs. No Livingston pacing in a hyperactive rhythm, dragging his bass guitar behind him. No Chase passed out in his beanbag. And definitely no Kaps staring at me in disbelief.

"Not alone," she repeats. "I am with the guitar man."

"My name is Rhodes."

Kaps steps up between us. "This guy plays guitar for me when I need it," she says. No shocker, here. It's been two whole minutes without Kaps being the center of attention.

Livingston stops his restless march. "Wow. That's what you call two red flags for our fan here." He raises his pointer finger.

"One, this is someone who's Furor and doesn't know her own kind. And second, she called you a guitar man."

"You still only have one finger raised," I say.

"That's not the point." Livingston stands beside Furor Girl and gestures toward the exit. "Hey, look! Here's the way out. How about you go there?"

Chase looks up. "Or come over here, kitten." He opens his mouth, drools, and then face-plants again.

I point at Chase. "You keep your hormones in check." Next I round on Livingston. "No one's kicking her out. She's been through something." Finally, I turn to Kaps. "Give her some breathing room, got it?"

Kaps huffs and saunters off to sit across the space. There, the princess plunks onto a beanbag, pulls out her data pad, and starts a little social media break. *Fine with me.* I use the opportunity to step closer to Furor Girl. When I speak again, I take care to gentle my voice. "Are you running away?"

Furor Girl nods. "But no longer. Now I shall follow you for a time."

"That's cool." I smile so hard, my face hurts a little.

Kaps rises while waving her data pad around. "Rhodes? May I have a word?"

There's a long moment where I want to tell Kaps to buzz off. But she's my responsibility. And Kaps with a data pad usually means something terrible. Last time, it meant she'd gotten a new bounty on her head from L'Griffe … as in the very group that just tried to blow us up on stage.

In other words, I'm talking to Kaps.

I scan the guys. "Keep an eye on the new girl, will ya?" Livingston and Chase say nothing, which I expect. Bash nods, and that's exactly what I want. He's the only responsible one anyway. Turning, I focus on Furor Girl. "You'll hang out here, alright?"

"Stay with you."

That reply makes me unreasonably happy. It's all I can do not to sprout my dragon wings and fly around the tent. "Good," I say. "I'll be right back."

Kaps saunters out the tent flap. I follow along, with one phrase reverberating through my being.

This better be good.

14

ZINNIA

*R*hodes of the Guitar Men leaves. That is a shame. The other Furor here smell sweaty and foul. Not like Rhodes of the Guitar Men. His scent is all moonlight and spices.

I edge toward the exit and some fresher air when a new and especially foul stench strikes me. Ick. Inhaling deeply, I find the stench comes from the Furor man laying upon the round sack. I take a closer look. Sure enough, a greenish color glistens on his skin. I have seen this happen to some of my handlers, often after one of their human holidays when they take in too much drink.

Their friend is sick. Perhaps that is why the other Furor are acting so quiet and odd.

I set my hand above the sick Furor's head and summon my magic. Across the tent, a Furor drums on his legs. That is enough. Focusing in on the rhythm, I access my powers. Energy flows through me. I set my hand above the sick Furor's head. Magic churns along my palm. I set it loose. A haze of power cascades toward the ill dragon man.

As the magic settles onto the ill Furor's head, the green color fades from his skin. Soon he rolls onto his side, smacks his lips and snores.

I look to the other Furor. "Your friend is healed," I proclaim.

The fidgety one stops his pacing. "Red flag number three," he murmurs. Not that I know what that means. But it seems this particular Furor tribe values flags.

The Furor who'd been drumming pauses. "How did you do that?"

"Magic," I say. "Isn't it obvious?"

"I got that," says the drummer Furor. "But not a lot of us can wield that much magic. You healed him really fast."

I stare at him and his friend for a long minute. Healing their friend did nothing to improve their states of mind. Clearly, these Furor are not as friendly as Rhodes of the Guitar Men. Just thinking about him makes my insides squirm in a pleasant way. Meanwhile, the other Furor stare at me with their mouths hanging open. They seem to lack basic knowledge of how to interact with other Furor. Perhaps my presence upsets them somehow.

I nod once to myself. That must be it. I can't be the only Furor who is overwhelmed by so many others being near. These three need their privacy.

A memory appears. Rhodes of the Guitar Men talked about meeting up later at something called the *bus*. I saw many signs for that before. I shall follow them and detect the correct spot based on Rhodes' scent.

With the decision made, I leave the tent and rejoin the crowd. Good news—there are not so many people as before. The sun has set, coloring the sky in shades of red and orange. The voice sounds again.

"Hey, you Trance-a-dancers! The big show starts in five minutes. Hustle off to the main stage."

I watch the flow of the crowd. Indeed, they are all following signs that read, *main stage*. I take a different route and head toward the direction of the buses. There are fewer people this way, which is calming.

Soon I step out onto a large swath of desert covered in odd coaches. I remember these from my book. These appear different, but humans may alter things over time. Metal coaches must be the same as buses. I catch the barest hint of moonlight and spices. That is Rhodes of the Guitar Men. Excellent. The scent is strongest at the metal coach marked with the words Cool Daze on the side. Strange, but the scent is strongest here. Unfurling my wings, I fly up onto the top of the coach.

It is cool and sweet atop the metal contraption. For a moment, I scan the horizon. Somewhere out there wait Killian and my handlers. Am I wrong to abandon them? The answer appears in a flash.

They lied to me.

Any one of the Furor I met today could be the Vessel of the Future. I do not wish to go back on my word, but neither will I lose my life without full understanding. Of course, I wish my family to return, but if I was told untruths about the Furor, one question remains.

What else have they lied to me about?

No, I shall wait until I have more answers. And if Killian and my handlers come after me? I welcome the chance to confront them. I have nothing to fear.

With that realization, all emotion seeps from my body. Sleep winds through my soul. I curl into a ball atop the cool metal roof. My tail loops around me. This feels familiar. My happiest moments are lounging outside my cave. This is the same thing, only that sweet smell of moonlight and spices is here as well. My muscles loosen and I drift off into a peaceful rest.

15

RHODES

Kaps leads me back to our stage area. Sure enough, it's deserted. Once there, she holds up her data pad for me to see. The screen is covered in a bunch of messages from a guy named Gage. I blink, not believing what I'm seeing.

"Is that Gage Beaufort?" I ask.

"Sure."

"And you're texting with him." *I can't believe this.*

"Yes, I can sing songs *and* text people."

"That's not what I mean. Gage Beaufort is the heir apparent to the L'Griffe crime family. You've got to be kidding."

"How else do you think I discover what they're after? They think I'm a mercenary named Lucille."

I press my palms against my eyes. "That is such a terrible idea, I don't even know where to start."

"Don't get all judge-y on me. I got a lead on Pandora's box. It's nearby and I'm going after it."

"You're kidding, right?"

"Why would I joke?"

"One word, Kaps. Bomb." I make an explosion noise and throw my hands apart, just to emphasize the the danger here.

"Please." Kaps holds the data pad against her chest like it's armor. "This is my fun. Let me have it."

I lower my hands. "Let's be honest here. If you want to start some kind of secret club to compete with L'Griffe, that's fine. Your parents would be cool with that."

Kaps narrows her eyes. "Meaning, what?"

"You don't have to fake up a band. There's no reason for you to sing."

"But I love singing."

I fix her with my most serious look. "Really?"

A long pause follows. Kaps knows what I mean here. She only started singing after Zin died.

"Don't bring *her* into it," snaps Kaps. No question who her is in this chat. *Zin.*

"It's not my favorite subject, either. I'm only trying to help."

"And I'm only trying to leave while giving you a heads up."

I rake my fingers through my hair. When Kaps gets this *treasure fever*, there's no talking her out of it. And I can't keep her safe if she's running after L'Griffe.

An option appears. I saw a flash of Huntress after the bomb went off. Could she still be hanging around, only invisible in her glass dragon form?

One way to find out.

I cup my hand by my mouth. "Huntress? Huntress, are you here?"

A few yards away, Huntress materializes. She wears black body armor and a wary look in her violet eyes. "Here," she says simply.

Kaps gasps. "How long have you been lurking around?"

"I came when I detected the explosion," answers Huntress.

"After the explosion?" I ask. "That kind of detection magic is tricky… assuming it's even possible."

"I'm a glass dragon." Huntress shrugs. "We specialize in the impossible." She rounds on Kaps. "You want to hunt Gage?"

"I want Pandora's box."

Huntress sets her hands on her hips. "I agree with you. We'll go together."

"Really?" Kaps beams.

Huntress raises her fist. "Sister power." The two share a fist-bump.

Knots of anxiety unwind inside me. *Great.* If Huntress teams up with Kaps, that's ideal. Even Tempest and Portia would agree that Kaps is now safe. My thoughts circle back to the Furor Girl I left in the tent. Is she all right? I take a few steps away from Huntress and Kaps. "Looks like you two have this. Be sure to reach out to your parents before you go."

Kaps frowns. "But you just talked to them."

"They want you home for your birthday," I explain. "All you need to do is reassure them you're on it. That would mean a a lot."

"Will do," says Kaps. There's a sneaky look on her face. I've seen that before. Kaps will do as I ask, but she'll cause trouble about it.

"You're really talking to Portia and Tempest, right?" I ask.

"Yes," says Huntress, which means this will actually happen.

"You heard Huntress," adds Kaps. "And I'll meet up with you at the next gig in Houston."

"It's San Antonio," I correct.

"That's what I meant," says Kaps brightly.

I stop my slow progression toward the exit. Maybe this isn't the best idea after all.

"Do not worry," says Huntress. "Princess Kappa Psi Phi Sigma will be safe with me." There are times when Huntress is all steely eyes and a firmly set jaw. Like now. It means she'll make something happen.

"Great," I say quickly. "See you at the next gig."

With that, I rush back to the prep tent.

16

RHODES

I race back to the tent, but it seems like my legs won't move fast enough. After what feels like way too long, I finally get back inside.

Furor Girl isn't there.

I scan Chase, Bash, and Livingston. They're all perched on bean bags, oblivious.

"Guys," I say. "Where is the new girl?"

"The *red flag fan?*" asks Livingston.

"You know that's who I mean." Sometimes, Livingston goes slowly to annoy me. Makes me want to yank off his mask and jam it down his throat. "What happened to her?"

"She fixed Chase and left," replies Livingston.

"And you just let her go?" I ask.

Livingston shrugs. "Sure."

White-hot rage heats my blood. "I asked you to keep an eye on her. It's obvious that she'd been through something bad. How could you be such a pack of dicks?"

Bash rises. "Calm down, Rho."

But that's the last thing I want to do. My eyes flare demon red with rage. "I've had it with you guys. You can strike the set on your own. I'll crash on the bus." Turning, I march out of the tent before I start punching someone. Mostly Livingston. The trio call out after me. I pay no attention.

She's gone.

Furor Girl.

This shouldn't tear at my soul, but it does. Maybe I've been babysitting Kaps for too long, I don't know. After pushing through what's left of the crowd, I reach the bus, let myself in, and slip into my bunk. The main concert starts. Cheers from the crowd echo through the air. Music pounds so loudly, the windows rattle. Odd noises reverberate from the roof.

I pause. *Wait a second.* Did I really hear something from above?

A full minute passes.

No new noises come from the bus' roof. Shaking my head, I curl under my blanket. It's been a hell of a day. Those sounds must have been my imagination. Despite the music and excitement, I fall asleep super fast.

And my dreams are strange to say the least.

In my night visions, I join Sienna back in her days as a human, playing her cello to a packed house. The place is all low ceilings, lots of wood, and an audience jammed around small square tables. As always when Sienna performs, she holds a cigar in her teeth. Sienna plays for a minute or so and then pauses. No question what happens next. Story telling is always a big part of Sienna's act.

"Got another one for you," says Dream Sienna.

The crowd applauds. They love her tales.

"Did I tell you the one about the time my dragon son got his life turned upside down?" asks Sienna. "It's a doozie." She then explains about my life in great detail, and it's all about Furor Girl.

I want to remember everything, but Sienna's words slip from my mind the moment she speaks them.

17

RHODES

I awaken to the quiet hum of the bus and Chase's snoring. We're on the road. *Funny.* I slept so soundly, I didn't hear Nikki fire up the bus. Must have needed the rest. After sliding out of my bunk, I head to the mini bathroom at the back. With each step, more of my anger from last night returns.

How could they let Furor Girl go?

And why does it bother me so much?

I reach the mini bathroom and pause. Someone wrote on the door in lipstick: *Piss Palace.* How lovely. And the handwriting isn't familiar. Shaking my head, I glance over at Chase's bunk. A girl's leg hangs out the edge. Turns out, Chase wasn't the one snoring. There's someone in there with him. She must be the lipstick artist.

Not for the first time, I plot to fire Chase. He isn't our regular lead guitarist, but the last guy quit. Sadly, word's gotten around that this isn't a fun gig. It took forever to find Chase in the first place. I thought we could look past the fact that we was lazy, older and smelled like booze.

What a mistake.

I step inside the mini bathroom and do my business. It's a

small space, so I can't help but catch a look at myself in the mirror. My mouth is thinned to an angry line and there's no question why.

Furor Girl is gone.

Rheeeeee! A squeal of a police siren slices through the air.

Livingston pounds on the door. "We're getting pulled over. You have to do something." I can't help but notice that he doesn't even ask where Kaps is. And this is her band. The guys used to ask questions when our lead singer would disappear. Now they just know she'll show up right before she has to go on stage.

I push the door open. "I'm on it."

"We're pulling over," announces Nikki. She's a badass human driver from Mumbai who wears saris and takes no prisoners. Normally, we don't allow any mortals to hang around with us. But some humans are fully aware that dragon shifters exist. Nikki is part of that group, and she's awesome.

The bus lurches as it pulls over to the side of the road. I do the world's fastest job of pulling on fresh jeans and a Cool Daze T-shirt. Once done, I step up to the front of the bus. Nikki's a grandmotherly type… if your grandma takes no crap and loves diner food. She reaches over and pulls the front bus door open. Outside there stands a human man in jodhpurs. He's tall with slicked back gray hair and reflective sunglasses.

I force on my best *innocent face*. "What's the problem, sir?"

"You have a girl," snaps the officer.

My thoughts immediately go to Chase. *That bastard.* "We do." Angling my head, I let out a whistle. "Chase, get up here."

Chase hustles to the front of the bus. He's only wearing jockey underwear. *Classy.* "Hey, guys."

"This is Chase." I hitch my thumb toward my mostly-nude bandmate. "He can tell you all about the girl."

"How did you get her?" asks the officer.

Chase blinks quickly. I've seen this look on him before. He's not quite awake yet. "We..." Chase lets out a long yawn. "Met after the show."

Muscles tighten along the officer's throat. This guy is getting angrier by the second. "Let me try again," says the officer. "How did you get her on *the roof?*"

"What?" asks Chase. "Sharyn is in my bunk."

A voice calls up from the back of the bus. "My name is Shawna."

"Right," says Chase. "Shawna. That's what I said."

On reflex, I pull on my ear. *Did he just say roof? I think he said roof.*

"Wait a second," I say. "Let me take a look."

My heart thuds against my rib cage as I step off the bus. Sure enough, someone clings on to the roof of our bus.

It's Furor Girl. She's sitting on the bus' roof with her face tilted up to the sun.

We are in so much trouble.

"Let me try one last time," says the officer. "What's the girl doing on your roof?"

"I don't know. I'll find out."

Livingston takes this opportunity to join me outside the bus. The good news is that he's wearing sweats instead of underwear only. The bad news is that he's still wearing that creepy ghost mask. Livingston points to the roof. "Wow, that's like trespassing or something. Should we shoot her down?"

"Why, you got a gun on the bus, son?" asks the officer. The way he asks the question, I know the correct answer. It's also good that it happens to be true.

"We have no firearms on the bus," I say.

"No," agrees Livingston. "But we could buy a tranquilizer gun or something. I once saw a movie where—"

"Son." The officer steps closer to Livingston. "Is there something wrong with your face?"

"What do you mean?" asks Livingston.

When I next speak, I take care to use my most warning tone. "Take off the mask."

"But I never take it off." Livingston does that thing where he realigns the mask so we can better see his eyes. In this case, it's now clear that his expression is one of pleading. "I've gone eight months with a mask on."

Bash steps off the bus. Never been happier to see him. "The mask goes off," he declares.

While that drama plays out, I scale up to the roof, using the front hood as leverage. As I climb over the windshield, Nikki glares at me. "I don't get paid enough for this." She has a clipped accent that makes every statement sound extra official.

"No, you don't," I agree. "You'll get a raise."

Nikki grins. She's gotten three raises so far this month. Deserves every one of them, too. With that decided, I hoist myself onto the roof.

There she is.

Furor Girl.

She crouches atop of the bus, her hands curled directly into the metal. My brows lift. *So that's how she stayed in place.* Plus, her tail spikes directly into the roof itself. The bus is a little trashed, but she's here. *Furor Girl.* My body feels so light, it's like I could soar off into the clouds.

We stare at each other. The moment lasts too long.

"What's your name?" I ask.

"I am the Vessel of the Future," she replies. "You are Rhodes of the Guitar Men."

"Yeah, that's right." I crawl closer. "You have to get down, oh Vessel of the—" I huff out a breath. "I can't call you that. How about Ves?"

"That is odd, but satisfactory, oh Rhodes of the Guitar Men."

"Just call me Rhodes."

She tilts her head, considering. "No. You are a stranger. If you weren't Furor, I wouldn't have followed you at all. Soon I may return to my cave."

"Cave." My heart sinks. *Cave*—what does that mean? Some kind of Furor commune on Earth? There are a lot of little settlements around.

She gives me a small smile. "But I shall travel with you for a time."

I can't help but grin back. *She's staying.* "That's great. But you see, we guitar men don't sit on the roofs of buses."

"Why not? It is rather pleasant."

"Well, we have to exist with humans, and they don't understand such things."

"Ah, you mean the flashing little wagon with the strange man in puffy pants. Have I upset that human?"

"Yes, I'm afraid so." I glance over the side of the bus. Sure enough, Officer Anxious waits by the front door. His hand now rests on the pommel of his gun. Not good.

Ves looks between me and the police man. "He is afraid of me."

Down below, the officer now unholsters his weapon. Not that he could hurt us—I'm too well trained for that—but an incident like this would mean exposing the truth about dragon shifters. We can't let that happen. Magic users would have to haul over here and wipe this human's memory. That's a hassle.

Ves lowers her voice to a whisper. "Beware. Humans can be evil."

"Look, Ves. We need to get down before the nice human policeman shoots up the place."

Ves lifts her chin. "I have battle training with all kinds of weapons. I fear no human." She tilts her face back to the sun. "And it is pleasant up here."

"Yet inside the bus is much more comfortable, I swear."

Livingston yells toward us. "Are you all right up there? Do I need to step in and kick her ass?"

"No way," I call back to him. "I'm handling this." I turn to Ves. Clearly, she wants to stay here in the sunshine. Not that I blame her. *So what do I have that can lure her down?*

In the end, I say the first thing that comes to mind. "We have snacks on the bus."

"Snacks?"

"Food."

"Protein bars?" She scrunches up her nose in a way that says, *protein bars suck.*

"No, better stuff. We have some crackers, I think. And maybe old Vernors."

She frowns. "I will not feast on old human named Vernor."

"No, it's just a drink."

"It does not sound as pleasant as sitting up here."

I lace my fingers behind my neck and think. So far, I've tried comfort and food. Neither will get Ves off the bus.

Closing her eyes, Ves begins to hum. The smallest melody sounds from her. I recognize the tune instantly. It's the first line of what I played last night, only without words.

An idea appears.

"That music," I offer. "Did you like when I played it last night?"

Her gaze snaps to mine. She gives me the barest of nods.

"My guitar is in the bus. If you come inside, I'll play it for you again."

She offers we a full smile and it's nothing less than dazzling. "I would like that, oh Rhodes of the Guitar Men."

I exhale. "That's great." I offer her my hand. "Now we need to slowly climb down the bus so we don't spook our nice friend Mister Officer."

She stands, extends her wings and soars down to land on her feet. The policeman almost falls over in shock.

"What was that?" asks the officer.

Scrunching up my mouth, I trying to think of what possible

explanation would work. To the officer, Ves just floated to the earth without benefit of wings or any visible equipment.

"I'll be right down to explain," I call.

"Musicians," grumbles the officer. "You kids are up to something. I should haul you all in."

"There's a really good explanation," I add. "One minute."

This time, I head down extra slowly. That buys me time to think of some way to explain everything. After all, the officer is right to be suspicious. We're really a bunch of dragon shifters hauling around an adrenaline junkie princess who wants to take on a secret band of mafiso dragons.

At some point, our luck is bound to run out.

18

ZINNIA

*T*his is confusing.

I now stand before the bus. Rhodes of the Guitar Men said this position would calm the police human in his puffy pants. Yet the officer mortal does not seem comforted.

I step closer to the police human. "I shall not attack you." Leaning in, I take a good inhale of his scent. The acidity of fear is overwhelming. "There is no reason to be afraid."

Rhodes shimmies down the front face of the metal wagon. Not sure why he did that. Any Furor could simply leap as I did.

"You..." stammers the police human. "You're..."

I tilt my head. "What?"

"Only wearing a T-shirt," says a girl from inside the bus.

"Shut up, Sandy." The speaker is the guitar player I healed yesterday.

"It's Shawna, You Dick." I make note of his formal name. *You Dick.* This suits the once-ill guitar player well.

Rhodes steps up beside me. "Here's the deal, officer. We're a rock and roll band called Cool Daze. Have you heard of us?"

The officer shakes his head slowly. He is not pleased.

"Our friend here is from the Cirque du Patate," says *my Rhodes.*

Not sure when I decided to call him *my Rhodes,* but it suits. And I can always use his formal and correct greeting in public.

"And?" asks the officer human.

"She performs on stage at all our shows," says my Rhodes.

The police human rubs his chin. "Cirque du Patate. Where is this show?"

Patate means potato, not that I state this part. My Rhodes is trying to calm the officer human. Perhaps the mortal is a fan of starch.

"It's all part of the Cool Daze band," answers my Rhodes. "We next perform in San Antonio, two days from now. You can check."

The officer man sighs. "Fine. I'll let you go this time." The human looks to me. "But ride *inside* the bus, little lady."

I bow slightly. "I shall vow to do this, sir."

The police man sniffs. "French people," he murmurs under his breath. That seems to explain everything to him. Which confirms something I've always suspected.

Humans are rather strange.

My Rhodes sets his hands on my shoulders and guides me inside the metal wagon. Everyone else marches in behind us. Soon, the vehicle lurches to life as we return to the road. The motion is so unexpected, I almost fall over. My Rhodes presses against me, holding my body in place. It is a very nice and squirmy sensation. Only I do not know my Rhodes too well, so I step out of his touch.

I miss him the moment he's far away. Clearly, I need more rest or food. My mind isn't working correctly. How can I miss someone I just met?

My Rhodes walks on ahead. Once he reaches the end of the metal wagon, he pauses. "You can take my bunk, if you like." He gives me a sweet smile. "How long do you plan to stay?"

I frown, considering this news. "I do not need to return for days." I could add that I should return to my handlers on my birthday, but I do not. Besides, I'm not even certain I *shall* return. There are answers to gather first.

"Is anyone looking for you?" The way my Rhodes asks the question, I feel like there is some meaning I do not know.

"I have human handlers."

My Rhodes lowers his voice. "Handlers. I don't know what that means."

"I am hiding from my humans for a time. But I must be honest. If my humans see you, they may think you have taken me. They could try to kill you. Is this of concern?"

"Not too much," says my Rhodes. "I'm a trained warrior."

Raising my voice, I address the group. "Is that how you *all* feel? There is no concern for human attackers?" I scan each face on the bus. None seem worried about my handlers.

How interesting.

At last, the driver breaks the silence. "Rhodes is a badass," she declares. "We're all fine."

"Badass?" I ask.

"I'm a pretty good warrior." My Rhodes gives me a sly look. There is a challenge in that stare. *So exciting.* I rarely get to spar with anyone who isn't a human.

"I am tempted to see what you can do," I state.

He opens his arms in a way that says, *I'm here.* So I launch into some rapid fire moves.

First, I try jamming my knuckles into his throat.

My Rhodes grabs my wrist, blocking the movement. His motions are so fast, they appear as a blur. Good, but that might have been luck, as Gracie would say.

So I try to kick his head. It isn't easy in such a cramped space, but I manage.

My Rhodes blocks my leg with his elbow. Clever.

Next I crouch low and kick forward. This should take out my Rhodes at the ankles.

Yet my opponent uses the movement against me. I end up on my back with my Rhodes laying on top of me. Once again, the sensation is rather pleasant.

"You *are* well trained," I say.

"That's right," says my Rhodes. "As are you."

He and I then share another long look. Although his face has the strong lines of a proven warrior, his green eyes sparkle with excitement. I think back to how my handlers would press their mouths together when they thought I wasn't looking. I never understood the appeal. But with my Rhodes? I wonder what it would be like.

My Rhodes rises, breaking the moment. "Like I said, here's my bunk. It's nothing fancy."

I pull back fabric. A small cubby sits inside. "What do you do in here?"

"Sleep."

"Not as a dragon, though, surely?"

"Only as a human."

"How long do you stay in this weak and mortal form?" All of a sudden, I have nothing but questions for him.

"Most of the time, especially on Earth."

I purse my lips and think. For some reason, these Furor masquerade as humans and live among them. I turn my attention to the bunk structure. Leaning forward, I press my hands against the bottom. The texture is springy. "This *would* be comfortable for a human."

"You sleep as a dragon?"

"I spend most of my time in my perfected form."

A nearby curtain pulls back. The other girl on the bus pops her head out. "What kind of crazy are you people?" she asks.

I frown. Is this some kind of odd greeting for her mortal

tribe? I remember the name that was mentioned before. Gracie taught me that it's very important to address people properly.

"Greetings," I say slowly. "Oh Shawna of the Chase You Dick." Laughter echoes through the bus. I set my hand over my mouth. "Is something humorous? Did I do the greeting incorrectly?"

The boy wearing a mask pops his head out from his own bunk. "She got you, Shawna."

"Shut up." The girl pulls back the curtain and is gone.

I am unsure what just happened, but it seems that whatever took place, I won a verbal battle. And I do so love to be victorious.

"What would you like to do?" asks my Rhodes. "Sleep? Eat?"

"I shall explore this bunk structure." I slip inside. It looks snug and feels cozy. "This is very comfortable. I shall sleep now."

And so I do sleep for a time. But all too soon, voices awaken me.

"You can't keep her here. We have no idea who she is." That's the boy with the mask speaking.

"All the more reason to keep her," says my Rhodes. "We all agree to do the minimum—food, hotel, shower, and clothes."

"Clothes are optional." That is Chase You Dick.

"Shut the hell up, Chase. You've got Shawna." That's the large man who carries small sticks. I think he is the drummer. It will take time to learn all their names and how to formally address them.

"I *had* Shawna," says Chase You Dick.

"We can't keep regular mortals on the bus," says my Rhodes.

"Only because you've got a bat shit crazy Furor in here." That's Chase You Dick once more.

"Look, you know the rules," says my Rhodes. "Mortals don't stay. Except for you, Nikki."

"Damned straight," says the driver. "Hey, my favorite diner is coming up."

"They're all your favorite diner," says my Rhodes.

"Same difference. Want to get your girl some food?" asks the driver.

"Yes, thanks." That's my Rhodes.

Chase You Dick speaks next. "She can't go into public in just that shirt."

"I've got it covered," says my Rhodes. "Kaps left some stuff under her bunk. Looks like Ves might be the same size."

Footsteps sound down the main aisle of the metal wagon. My Rhodes opens the curtain. I sit up and speak.

"I will eat in this restaurant for I am hungry. But you still must play on your guitar for me. And I'll only wear another's clothes if I approve."

"Heard all that, did ya?" asks my Rhodes.

"Yes, I miss nothing."

"I'm starting to realize that." And my Rhodes seems rather pleased by this fact.

And for some reason, it overwhelms me with joy to see him so happy. It is wondrous enough that I forget I have only five days left to live.

19

RHODES

*N*ikki parks at the Lone Star Diner. While the rest of the band goes in for a bite, I get to work on finding something for Ves to wear. Turns out, finding her an outfit isn't easy. To begin with, there's the awkwardness of going through Kaps' stuff. I asked Nikki to do it, but she says she's not interested, even when I promised her another raise. And there's no way I'll let the other guys dress my Furor Girl.

Which leaves it up to me. I open the drawer under Kaps' bunk. Up top, there's a notebook marked *L'Griffe*. Beside it sits another box labeled *pictures*. I set those aside and get to some actual clothes. This results in a ton of questions.

Would Ves like a glittery pink halter top? *No, disco is dead.*

Or maybe this onesie romper? *She's not six. Another no.*

Next there's a lot of underwear that I'd rather not know anything about. Eventually, I do find jeans, a regular non-sparkly T-shirt and some basic underthings. By the time I'm done, my pulse is speeding and sweat drips down my back. It all adds up to one fact.

Dressing females is really stressful. How do girls manage this every day?

With the outfit in hand, I head back to Ves' bunk. I lean toward the curtains. "Are you awake?"

The curtains open a crack. Ves' eyes are visible through the break. "Yes."

"I got you some things to wear."

Ves opens the curtains fully. I can't help but grin. She looks so cute and sleepy. My Furor Girl takes the jeans and T from my hands and turns them over.

"These are acceptable," she states.

Those three words warm me with an unreasonable amount of happiness. "Good."

Ves picks up bra with her thumb and forefinger. "And what is this contraption?" The way she holds the item, it's like it's from space.

"It's a bra. You use it to—" I mime holding up my invisible breasts and stop myself before getting too far. This is beyond embarrassing. "You really don't know what a brassiere is for?"

"Is it a bra or a brassiere? And why were you making those hand gestures before?"

In an odd act of kindness from the universe, Nikki steps into the bus. "Now where did I put my sunglasses?" she asks to no one in particular. To my eyes, it's like there's a halo around her. Or an aura of beautiful timing. In other words, I'm so happy to see Nikki that I could shout with joy.

I cup my hand by my mouth. "Nikki, a little help here?"

Nikki sets her fists on her hips. "With what?"

Ves juts her arm out of the bunk and holds out the bra so it dangles above the aisle. "I do not understand this thing."

There's a long pause as Nikki looks between me, Ves, and the bra.

Come on, Nikki. Help a guy out.

"No, sir," Nikki declares at last. "You do not pay me enough."

I cross my fingers behind my back. "Another raise?"

"Still not enough."

For her part, Ves just keeps staring at me. She's all big blue eyes and innocent confusion. My face burns about eighteen shades of red.

"You know what?" I ask. "Let's forget about that for now." I reach for the bra.

"Wait." Ves pulls the garment out of my grasp. "I think I have it. The cups are for my breasts."

"Yeah." And the underwear are for—

Ves gives me the side eye. "I know all about underwear."

One part of my brain—the logical side—thinks that Ves must have lived with regular Furor when she was a girl. That would explain knowing about underwear and not a bra. The rest of my head—the feeling side—just screams to get the hell off this bus. Now.

Ves tilts her head. "Are you all right, Rhodes of the Guitar Men? You look ill."

"I'm fine." Turning, I scoop some flip flops from Kaps' bunk and set them on the floor before Ves. "These are for your feet."

"I know that as well. Are you certain you're not sick?"

"Nope. Fine."

Ves whips her T-shirt off and I turn around before getting a look. All right, I got a small look because I really couldn't help it. She's gorgeous. However, the movement means I'm no longer staring at a line of bunks. Nope. Now I'm looking at Nikki, who still stands at the front of bus. Her sunglasses are now gripped in her hand.

Nikki shakes her head. "You're blushing, Rhodes. Didn't know you had it in you."

"Nice," I say. "Glad you found your sunglasses. Why don't you go to the diner? That place has amazing burgers."

I feel pressure on my shoulder. It's Ves, tapping me from behind. She's fully dressed now, thankfully. "Burgers?" she asks. "Is that the lovely smell on the air?"

I take in a deep breath. Sure enough, she's right about the scent. Burgers and grease. "Yes, that's right."

Ves' face brightens. "Let us get some red sandwiches."

"Sure." That's what I say, but in my head? My logical side kicks in again. In Furonium, we call burgers *red sandwiches*. For us, we make a very rare and thin patty and serve it plain on special bread. Which settles things. Ves must have lived in the dragon realm at some time. Rapid fire questions rattle through my head.

What happened to her?

How did she end up in the desert?

Who are those humans that are after her?

There's so much to wonder about, but it's too early to press for answers. After all, I just talked the girl off the roof of my bus. She definitely needs a meal before I interrogate her.

Ves grabs my hand, pulling me toward the front of the bus. "Red sandwiches," she sighs. "I can not wait."

And she's not the only one who's anxious. Something tells me that Ves is in trouble. I need answers if I'm going to keep her secure.

Because anything other than safe is simply unthinkable.

20

ZINNIA

*M*y Rhodes and I step across a strange space. The ground is made of packed bits of stone. Many different metal wagons surround a small building. A sign reads, *Lone Star Diner.* Inside the structure, many humans sit around small tables.

The crystal ball appears in my mind once more. A memory surfaces. I sit at a golden table. There are others beside me, only I can't see their faces. We eat red sandwiches from white plates. I try to catch any detail, but the image is gone as quickly as it appeared.

"Ves, are you okay?" asks my Rhodes.

"Yes."

"You stopped walking."

"Oh, I did not realize that." My shoulders slump with sadness. It was arrogant to think I could leave my cave and spend time with others. I can't even walk to get food without memories overwhelming me.

My Rhodes entwines his fingers with mine. His touch is calming and warm. "Ready to go when you are," he says softly. Together, we move forward.

There's no avoiding the truth. Holding hands with my Rhodes makes me feel much better. His touch is a good mixture of familiar, new, and comforting. With each step, I feel more secure in my decision to leave my cave. There is so much I haven't seen and done. Or, because of what happened to my memory, perhaps I simply don't remember what I've done.

That is the key.

I must recall everything.

My Rhodes rubs his thumb in a gentle arc over the back of my hand. An idea appears. My handlers always warned me not to trust outsiders. Sadly, my time may be limited. Only five days remain. I must be bold. Surely, I can trust my Rhodes with a little more information. Perhaps he can help me remember.

My life is my own. Maybe I am not a Vessel of the Future after all.

Crack! A noise sounds behind me.

Looking back, I see another fissure has opened on the loop of stone around my tail.

I take that as a very good sign indeed.

21

ZINNIA

*W*ith cautious steps, I cross the threshold to the diner building. Inside, a small podium stands by the door. The rest of the space holds a long counter as well as patchwork of tables. A handful of humans bend over their meals. Some of the mortals have worry demons gnawing on their ears. None have the rage demons that my handlers carry.

Excellent. This place is safe.

Some part of me notices the other folks from the metal wagon. They wave at me and my Rhodes while gesturing at empty chairs around their table. I start closer to them, but my attention gets locked on an empty table in the far corner. My eyes widen. A line of colored jars sit atop the shiny table.

Colored food? In jars? Amazing.

Leaving the others behind, I speed over to the far corner. I pick up the first jar. It is tall, squishy, and topped with a cone-like stopper. I lift it up, taking a deep inhale from the container.

A scent wraps around me.

Sweet.

Rich.

Delicious.

I grip the jar and squeeze. A bead of red appears on the top. I touch the substance and bring it to my lips. A burst of flavor erupts across my tongue. It is beyond anything I can imagine.

My Rhodes stands beside me. "That's catsup," he says. "Do you like it?"

I nod so quickly, the back of my neck hurts. This is a revelation. Who knew such tastes were possible? A flash of the crystal ball appears in my mind. Once more, that image of me sitting at a golden table appears in my mind. Just as quickly as it materializes, the mental picture vanishes.

I gaze upon the soft container in my hands. No question what to do next. Opening my lips, I tilt my head back and angle the catsup over my mouth. Then I squeeze the jar with all my strength.

While the small taste was delicious, a mouthful of the catsup is overwhelming in its perfection. My cheeks bulge with the delicious stuff.

Beside me, my Rhodes chuckles. "You like it, huh?"

After gulping down my mouthful, I nod speedily once more. That's when I refocus on the tabletop. Another container catches my attention. While the catsup was red, this one is yellow. Interest sparks in my chest. If the catsup was delicious, what awaits me in the yellow one? Something equally wonderful, certainly. Swiping the yellow container from the table, I repeat the process once again.

Open my mouth.

Hold the container above my lips.

Squeeze out everything I can.

A moment later, I realize my mistake. This stuff is disgusting. I drop the yellow container and set my hands over my mouth.

My Rhodes leans in closer. "Not a fan of mustard?"

I shake my head and force myself to swallow. "Ugh. That was foul."

A moment passes, while I realize a new person now stands

beside us. A stranger. She is thin as if her body were made from so many sticks bundled together. Her brown hair is tied behind her head. She wears a simple blue dress with the name Abby written on her chest. No demons gnaw upon her.

"Y'all gonna order?" Abby glares at the now-empty bottles. I look to my Rhodes. *Ordering.* That's some kind of ritual I'm not familiar with. Does it occur at the table, the long counter, or by the door where the little podium is set?

My Rhodes gives the woman a dazzling smile. "Absolutely." He sits down at the table and pats a seat beside him. I nod. It's clear that we order from the table. Good to know.

Once we're settled, Abby pulls out a small pad of paper from a pocket on her dress. "What do you want?" she asks.

"Two plain burgers," says my Rhodes. "And water."

"Sure thing, honey," says Abby. She scribbles onto her pad and steps away. Once Abby is gone, my Rhodes leans forward over the table. "I'm glad we got a table by ourselves."

"Oh?"

"We need to talk. I'm worried about you, Ves. Who are these humans that are after you?"

"I can handle myself."

"But I'm here as well. I'm a warrior who can help ... only that's not possible unless I understand what's happening."

I stare down at the tabletop, which is covered in deep and dirty scratches. I rub my thumbnail along the grooves and consider things. I do not want to leave my Rhodes. And he does not seem willing to depart from my side. I suspect that my vow to become the Vessel of the Future is a fraud, but I do not know this for certain. What if I make a poor decision and doom all the Furor?

Looking up, I scan Rhodes' face. He seems open and honest, but is that his true nature?

An answer appears in my mind. I do know one thing about

my Rhodes. *His music.* That song he played could not be created by a liar. I can trust him, at least in part.

"I will tell you some things, " I state at last.

My Rhodes lets out a long breath. "Anything you can share will be great." Reaching forward, he sets his hand atop mine. Once again, that wave of comfort moves through me.

This is right. I may begin to trust my Rhodes.

22

RHODES

*T*urns out, it's a good thing Ves decided to eat all the condiments at a random table. She picked the place farthest from the band. Now I can chat with Ves alone. In no time, Abby returns with our food. Ves pokes at the burger for a second or two. It's adorable. I pause on eating my own meal until she's comfortable.

"Do you want to get something else?" I ask.

Ves lifts her chin. "No, I shall try this burger."

Little by little, she leans over until she's at eye level with the bun. After her disaster with mustard, it looks like she isn't ready to jump into anything new. I don't blame her.

Eventually, Ves takes a bite. Her eyes widen.

"This is even better than catsup."

Her approval makes me beam. "I'm glad." She grins with her cheeks full of food. It's like she's like a sexy chipmunk.

Where did that come from? I'm supposed to be helping her, not hitting on her.

Although, I can't avoid noticing something.

I reach forward. "You've got a little …" I motion toward her mouth.

"What?" She swallows and damn, that's sexy too.

"A little bit of catsup stuck on your lip."

She licks her lips slowly. *This is torture.* "Did I get it?"

How I wish she did. "Nope, you missed it." I scooch my chair closer to hers. "Do you mind if I … ?"

"Not at all."

Reaching forward, I brush my fingers across her lower lip. The touch is electric. And her skin? Incredibly soft.

She leans in closer. "Thank you."

Once more, it's as if a bubble of awareness forms around us. The rest of the diner fades away. There's only me, Ves and the intense desire to kiss.

Focus, Rhodes. You need to get information, not lose your heart.

Clearing my throat, I slide my chair back to its original spot. "Mind if I ask a few questions?"

"You have my permission."

"Where did you live before this?"

"In a cave." She sips some water. "It was not far from where you played your concert." She picks up her burger again. "This is so good."

Which makes a nice lead-in to my next question. "What did you eat before?"

"Protein bars. They taste like paper."

Although we're pretty isolated, some topics are still sensitive. When I next speak, I take care to lower my voice. "You mentioned humans before. What can you tell me about them?"

"Mostly, they were handlers who guarded me and gave sparring practice."

I'm about to ask what they were guarding her for, but she starts licking her finger. It's incredibly distracting. All these years, I never really connect with anyone. And now? All I can think about is this girl. It's an effort, but I remind myself that Ves is here because she's in trouble, not looking for a date.

I take a big swig of water and get my thoughts back in line. "What are they preparing you for?"

She stares at the tabletop. "A ceremony."

"You can't say more?"

"Not yet." Ves pushes her plate away. "I don't really know you. These people raised me. I made promises to them. I have questions about things, but not enough yet to fully betray their trust."

"I understand," I say. "We need to get to know each other. That's cool."

Ves brings the water to her mouth again. Halfway to her lips, she pauses and takes in a deep breath. No question about it. Ves has caught a scent.

I inhale as well. There's a strange Furor approaching.

"You know who's coming, don't you?" I ask.

"Yes. You must depart. Lead the others away as well."

The diner door swings open. A scumbag Thorntail marches through. And not just any creep, but Killian, the eldest son of Oswine.

This is about to get ugly.

I'm not going anywhere.

23

ZINNIA

Killian storms into the diner. As always, he wears a too-tight suit on his massive frame. His gaze locks on me. The lines of his misshapen face pull tight with rage.

My Rhodes rises; every muscle in his body seems taught and ready to act. A low growl sounds from his chest. This is not a human sound. The dragon my Rhodes carries inside him must be close to the surface.

Killian's line of vision slowly flips between me and my Rhodes. Little by little, the anger in my lead handler's face eases into a simpering grin. That is to be expected. Killian is human, after all. Although mortals can not see our dragon forms, they sense us all the same. That easily explains Killian's change of attitude.

"Hello, there!" Killian waves at me.

How odd. That is not a proper greeting. I am always addressed as the Vessel of the Future. Killian is called the Son of Oswine. Perhaps the fear of a hidden dragon has made Killian forget his manners? Or could such greetings be particular to our training grounds? It is something to consider later.

Since this is not a proper greeting, I do not respond. Killian skulks over to our table. He extends his hand toward my Rhodes. "So good to see you."

Now it is my turn to look back and forth between two people. In my case, it is my Rhodes and Killian. Surprise prickles across my skin. "You two now each other?"

Killian takes a seat at the table. "Of course, we do. Long story."

My Rhodes stays standing. "Killian found my father after he was murdered."

My brows lift in surprise. *My Rhodes lost his father?*

"Please." Killian sets his meaty hand at his throat. "You don't think *I* had anything to do with *that?*"

"The inquest proved nothing," says my Rhodes. From his tone, it is clear that my Rhodes has suspicions about Killian. I knew my lead handler was a tough human, but could he actually murder a dragon? It seems hard to believe.

At this point, I realize that Killian is not the only one who has detected the angry energy from my Rhodes. Everyone in the diner has now stopped eating to stare. One human even drops her spoon into a bowl of stew, she is so frightened.

Any thoughts about Killian's past with my Rhodes must be set aside for now. On instinct, I reach over and touch my Rhodes on the arm. "Please sit down. We are scaring the mortals."

For a moment, Killian stares at the very spot where I touch my Rhodes' arm. That look of total rage overtakes his features once more.

"Killian, are you all right?" I ask.

Now, I know exactly why Killian is feeling *anything but right* at this time. I escaped from my desert camp. Now I travel with others of my kind. Killian should beg for my forgiveness while explaining why he lied about me being the last Furor. If anything, *I* should be the one enraged over so many falsehoods. Instead, Killian appears angry over by the casual way that I touch my Rhodes.

Good. At this point, any way to hurt Killian is something I value.

My Rhodes laces his fingers with mine. While staring at Killian, my Rhodes retakes his seat.

"Did you hear my question?" I ask Killian once more. "Are you quite well?"

"I'm fine." Killian forces on a smile that doesn't reach his eyes. "We've been so worried about you back at the training camp."

"Camp," repeats my Rhodes. "Explain that to me."

The way my Rhodes says the word *camp*, it's the way I might say *inspection day*.

"Of course, I can explain," says Killian. His knees bob in nervous rhythm under the table. "Our girl here is part of an elite warrior training program for the Thorntail tribe. All volunteers, of course." He looks to me. "Isn't that right?"

With my free hand, I drum my fingers on the tabletop. Killian is playing a game here; he pretends I am part of some formal program. Perhaps my lead handler still babbles out of terror from being near another dragon shifter.

It is possible.

Yet whatever the reason, I enjoy this nervous display from Killian. I shall allow it to continue.

"Killian is correct," I reply at last. "I made a vow."

"We've got the magic to prove it, don't we?" I know what Killian refers to here. *The cuff.* It must be how he tracked me here.

"Perhaps," I say. "Although I escaped that magic, right?"

"Escape you did," confirms Killian. "That was very naughty of you. It's time to return to camp and finish your training."

"Camp?" asks Rhodes. "I thought it was a cave."

Killian shifts nervously in his seat while his knees keep up that anxious rhythm. The sight is most entertaining. "Yes," Killian replies. "Our training grounds do include a cavern." He focuses on me. "Are you returning or what?"

"I do not think I shall." With my free hand, I slowly drag my plate back before me. The item makes a satisfying screech as it moves across the tabletop. I then pop the last bite of burger into my mouth. "Goodbye."

For a long moment, Killian stops all his fidgeting. He simply stares at me with his jaw open. Not sure what he expected would happen. This is not it, obviously.

"Won't you reconsider?" asks Killian at length.

"Perhaps." I take another swig of water. "If you explain why you lied to me. I am not the last of the Furor." I lean forward, eager to take in every detail of Killian's response. What he does here will tell me much. With any luck, Killian will reply with an open and honest answer, something that my Rhodes can hear as well.

This is not what happens.

Killian hops up to stand, his gaze flicking to the door. A low growl sounds from the parking lot. I know that sound.

Demons... Killian has summoned enemies here.

"I have an excellent explanation for you," says Killian. "But it's best discussed outside and in private. What do you say?" Killian stares at me, his small eyes wild with desperation. My lead handler wishes me to go outside now.

Prepare for disappointment, oh Son of Oswine.

I take care to pluck the napkin from the table, fluff it out, and daintily wipe each corner of my mouth. It remains enjoyable to make Killian squirm. "If you can not explain yourself here before my Rhodes, then I have no interest in your reply."

All the color drains from Killian's face. "My Rhodes?"

My Rhodes then hefts our joined hands onto the tabletop. "Hers," he says in a deadly voice. For some reason, that angry tone makes my heart flutter.

Killian glances to the door once again. "Ah, no trouble then. If you change your mind, you know where the training grounds are."

"That I do."

Without another word, Killian marches out the door. The human crowd in the diner long ago stopped staring, but the members of the band did not lose interest. Bash gets up from his chair and starts to head our way. My Rhodes waves him off; Bash retakes his seat. It is honorable that this drummer wishes to keep my Rhodes safe. I decide to give him a formal name.

"Bash of the Drummer Men is a good ally," I state.

"Yes, he is." My Rhodes refocuses to me. "How do you know Killian?"

"Killian led my training." There is more to say here, but I still know my Rhodes very little. In my situation, it is better to gain information than release it. "I am sorry to learn of your father."

"Thanks. It was a long time ago. Are your parents still living?"

It is a fair question, but it cuts to my soul. That crystal ball appears in my mind. Faces appear and disappear. "I do not remember." My Rhodes opens his mouth to ask a question, but I cut him off. Again I need to acquire knowledge here, not lose it. There is too much at stake.

"Is that the only way you know Killian?" I ask. "He found your father?"

My Rhodes eyes me for a long moment. No doubt, he is debating about pushing more on the topic of my memories. Seconds tick by before he replies.

"Killian is also the Master Dragon of Thorntails. That means he leads the tribe. Where I come from, that makes him a bit of a celebrity."

I shake my head in disbelief. "How does a human become Master Dragon?"

Now it is my Rhodes' turn to shake his head. "You don't see his tail?"

"No." I gaze at the door, as if Killian might still be there and show his tail to me. "He has a tail?"

"It's there, all right." My Rhodes taps his chin. "Killian

mentioned magic before—something that was cast when you made a vow?"

"That is correct."

"I bet there's an enchantment on you. It's hiding Killian's true nature."

Now, I knew about the tail cuff. The manacles. The crystal ball. But now an enchantment against seeing Killian's true nature? I roll my eyes. "I shall add that spell to the list."

My Rhodes' face turns angry as thunder. "How many spells did they cast on you?"

"I am unsure. My memories are blocked."

"That's outrageous! Back in Furonium, magic that alters other people's minds is very rare. It requires a ton of power and can only be done with royal permission."

The crystal ball reappears in my internal vision. When I speak again, my voice comes out low and dreamy. "Killian spoke truth. I made a sacred vow that saves those I love. As a result, most of my memories are gone, and that is my burden. Yet I can not break such a promise—can not fully turn my back on Killian—without understanding if doing so would hurt people I care about. Does that make sense?"

"It does. You've a good heart, Ves." His green eyes flare with determination. "But there must be some way to set you free from that guy and still keep your family safe. What do you know about the promise you made?"

"I try to remember, but it is very confusing." Releasing our joined hands, I rise. There are two reasons for this. One is that if I sit here with my Rhodes for too long, I'll tell him even more. It is still too early for that. The second is what awaits me outside. "Stay here, please. I shall return to the metal wagon alone."

My Rhodes frowns. "Killian's waiting for you outside. You know that, right?"

"Yes."

My Rhodes stands as well. "I scent demons on the air."

I nod. "Killian can summon them. No doubt, they will try to return me to my cave."

"That's not happening." My Rhodes tosses some greenish sheets of paper on the tabletop. "I'm going with you."

I frown. "I am not sure that is wise."

"You don't want to go with them, do you?"

"No." Faces flicker in the crystal ball. I can not make out details but I know one thing. *These are my family.* Will fully breaking my vow hurt them? Kill them? It is too early to say. Before I speak again, I take in a long and calming breath. "I am not ready to rejoin Killian. Not yet, anyway."

My Rhodes takes both my hands in his. "Then let me stand at your side."

Once more, there's a comfort in being near this man. And more than that. My Rhodes makes me feel safe. From the first second I first saw him, I felt secure that my Rhodes could destroy a bomb without hurting any humans.

I can trust him here as well.

"All right," I say.

My Rhodes waves to the table of band members. "Ves and I will head out first. Give us a few minutes." Chase You Dick keeps on chatting with the man with the mask. Bash of the Drummer Men does not join in their talk. Instead, he twists about in his chair and stares at my Rhodes warily.

Bash of the Drummer Men is right to be concerned.

This may not end well.

24

RHODES

*H*and in hand, Ves and I march out of the diner. My thoughts spin through everything I just learned.

Ves knows Killian.

No, she *more* than knows him.

Killian kept Ves in some kind of fake training program in a goddamn cave. And that evil Master Dragon has clouded her mind with spells. Ves doesn't even know her own past. And Killian's got something on her. Blackmail of some kind. There's a magical promise that keeps Ves tied to him.

Well, I'll smash that memory spell to bits, one way or another. Ves will not return to a cave with Killian of all dragons.

We step out the door and onto the parking lot. Mewling sounds reverberate from behind the bus. Pausing, I turn to Ves. "Are those…"

"Blood lion demons?" she finishes. "Yes. They start off as cat-sized and then expand from there." She shivers, as if remembering a past battle. "Killian likes to summon them for fights."

I crack my neck from side to side. "Blood lion demons. This will be interesting."

Ves pauses. "Oh, no."

"What?"

"Blood lions like to take a human hostage." She whirls around, scanning the front windows of the diner. "Where is Nikki?"

Mother of Hell. Not Nikki.

Grasping Ves' hand more tightly, I march around to the back of the bus. There lies Nikki, bound and gagged on the gravel. Killian has chosen a spot behind a line of rusted-out cars, so no one can see her.

The blood lions pace behind Nikki. Both have red fur, long fangs, and bat-style wings. The pair tower over me and Ves.

They're mammoth.

Actually, these two blood lions could probably *eat* a wooly mammoth and cough out a fur ball afterwards, complete with tusks.

Killian stands between the two monsters. "You really shouldn't have gotten involved, Rhodes. This is none of your affair."

I look down at poor Nikki. She writhes on the ground, trying to break free from the ropes on her wrists and feet. There's fire in her eyes as she tries to yell through her gag. If I get her out of this, I'm not sure there's enough money in the world to make this right.

I kneel beside her. "We'll rescue you, Nik." Her reply is a long and muffled tirade from behind the gag.

I get it. She's pissed.

"Our girl here," Killian gestures to Ves. "She knows what blood lion demons can do. So I'll give you a chance to end this peacefully without needlessly shedding more human blood."

Ves' chin wobbles. "You knew. You sent those other demons after Gracie."

My heart cracks. I'm not sure who Gracie is, but it's obviously someone Ves cares about. Yet another reason to hate Killian.

Killian shrugs. "You got too attached. That cost Grace her life. And you know what else?" He stares pointedly at me. "Forming more attachments is a good way to get others killed." Killian rounds on Ves once again. "Why do you think your precious family is still alive? If you recalled them in detail, you'd do something stupid. By erasing your memories, I'm doing you a favor."

A low growl erupts from Ves' chest as she changes into half-dragon form. Her skin covers over in scales. A crown of razor-sharp thorns encircles her head. Her hands elongate into powerful claws.

I've never seen a Thorntail to match her. As a rule, that tribe is built for sucking up and subterfuge. The most lethal they get is Killian in his dragon form, and he's more of a big lump than anything.

Ves' tail swipes behind her and I gasp. Why didn't I notice it before? Most dragons in Furonium have arrowhead-shaped ends on their tails, except one. Thorntails. Their dragon form ends in spiked club. Ves has their gray scales, yet she also has an arrow-head-shaped end to her tail.

Is this another spell? If so, why?

There's no time to wonder. The blood lions have spread their wings. One angles its jaws toward Nikki, getting ready to take my poor driver in its mouth.

That's not happening.

Ves leans back and lets out a roar.

Summoning up my power, I transform into my full dragon shape. I'm a long and muscular beast with a head of horns and a spiked spine. As a dragon, I can more fully access my Electrophus power. Magic churns through my limbs. I open my maw and set it loose.

Crack!

Lines of lightning spew from my jaws and tearing through the blood lions. The scent of charcoal fills the air. Both demons roar as they're incinerated. Moments later, all that remains is a handful of ash. I round on Killian.

"You're next," I growl.

Seconds pass as Killian's mouth grinds out silent words. "I had no idea you could do that."

"What you don't know about Electrophus dragons is a lot." I always suspected Killian had seen some—or all—of Father's death. Titan's body had signs of red magic on his skin, the same as they found on me. Father had been sabotaged in his last battle. Whatever Killian may have seen with Titan, it wasn't a full display of Electrophus powers.

Killian pulls a small cube from the folds of his suit coat. He presses the sides in an odd rhythm; the container expands into a large glass box. The unmistakable image of Pandora's starfall glows on its side.

I blink hard.

Shake my head.

Blink again.

The container is still there, gripped in Killian's meaty hands.

It can't be.

Yet it is.

Pandora's box.

25

RHODES

*B*efore us, Killian grips Pandora's box. I recall my last chat with Kaps. According to the princess, L'Griffe knew Killian had this magical item. When Kaps told me the news, I had my doubts. After all, something like Pandora's box is more legend than reality.

Turns out, L'Griffe knows their stuff. Killian grips the box's lid.

Now I've seen magical containers before. Opening Pandora's box will release a jet of colored enchantment and power.

I brace myself, waiting for the onslaught of magic.

It doesn't happen.

Instead, four little dots of magic lazily float up from the container.

Ves chuckles. "You've used up too much, Killian. What will four lonely specks do for you?"

The dots glow red with energy. For a few seconds, the spots of colored light whirl around Killian. For some reason, the sight reminds me of four mini-planets spinning about a dark sun. As the magic whirs faster, a pink haze surrounds Killian from head to toe.

Then the Master Dragon vanishes.

I stare at the spot where Killian disappeared. Red dots. That's what they found on my body after Zin was killed. Crimson magic was all over Titan as well. I'd always suspected that Killian saw Father's death. Was it more than that? Did Killian wield Pandora's box even then?

The Master Dragon have have done more than witness Titan's death. Killian may have caused it as well.

Rage unlike anything I've ever known whirls through my dragon's form. Electrophus power grows inside my body. I want to wipe out everything within a mile of this spot. Erase any sign that Killian had ever been here.

I open my dragon's maw, ready to release my revenge. Killian is no longer here, but like the day when I incinerated Titan's funeral boat, there is some comfort in any kind of action.

That's when small human hands brush along my dragon's neck. "My Rhodes?"

I tear my gaze away from the spot where Killian last stood. It's Ves. She stands before me in her human form and gently strokes my scales. When she speaks again, her voice is deep and calming. "My Rhodes."

My inner pull toward destruction fades. Instead, I sense a magnetic attraction to the girl before me. Not many Furor can derail a dragon who's in the throws of rage. Yet Ves did just that.

It's almost as if she's my rhana. Yet that can't be.

A new voice sounds beside me. "What the Hell are you doing, standing naked in the parking lot?" It's Nikki. She hands me a SpongeBob SquarePants towel while staring pointedly at the sky.

I look down. All my rage at Killian moves aside because somewhere along the line, I transformed back into my human state. Since I shredded my clothes when becoming a dragon, that means I'm now naked. I shoot a glance toward Ves. She's staring up at the sky as well. A cute pink shade colors her face.

Better get covered up.

I swipe the towel from Nikki. "SpongeBob?" I ask.

"I like the show," counters Nikki. "Now put it on."

I wrap the tower around my waist. "How did you get free?"

"Ves released me."

"And you're still here?" I asked. "I thought you'd run off."

"What is wrong with you? I drive a bus full of dragons. Is there a better job anywhere? No. Now, get back on board so we can hit the road."

Of course, I could get back on the bus, but I do love Nikki's admission that she loves her job. I decide to drag out the moment a little. "Tonight, we're staying at the San Antonio Sleepaway, right?"

It's a crappy hotel, but they don't mind when we shred the furniture with our tails. Not that I'm guilty of this, but Chase and Kaps can get carried away.

"Change of plans," declares Nikki. "No hotels. I know things."

I lift my brows. "You do?"

"Yes," states Nikki. "That Killian fellow is tracking you. No hotels. I know a place where we can camp."

Now, I'm pretty sure that Killian is tracking Ves using her tail cuff, but that will happen no matter where we go. After the recent blood lion disaster, I'm betting Killian won't come near us for a while. The bigger question is whether Ves wants to camp or not.

I turn to Ves. Unlike me, she never shifted into full dragon form, so she's still dressed. "What do you say?"

"My old cave was called a camp," explains Ves. "That would be a comfortable choice." She takes in a deep breath, as if ready to add something else. She doesn't, though.

"What is it?" I ask.

"I have made a decision," says Ves. "I shall call you *my Rhodes*. Officially."

I do a double-take. "My Rhodes? Officially?"

"I gave you that name in my mind before," explains Ves. "Now I shall speak it out loud."

The magnetic feeling between us grows even stronger. "I'd like that."

"What are you doing?" Nikki wags her finger at me. "Get on my bus and put on some clothes."

At this point, the band members rush up. "What happened?" asks Chase.

"Some demons came by and Rhodes killed them," declares Nikki. "Now everyone on the bus! We are not waiting around for more trouble."

I shake my head. *Nikki the bus driver. What a badass.*

26

ZINNIA

*a*s Nikki of the Bus Drivers requested, I file on the metal wagon along with the others. Once on board. I take a seat in the center area where there are tables. With any luck, Rhodes will slide in beside me. Happily, that is just what he begins to do when Nikki approaches.

"I want my SpongeBob towel back." Nikki points to the door which reads, *Piss Palace*. "Get dressed."

My Rhodes holds his hands up in a sign of mock defeat. It is a shame that he will change into full clothing again. I must admit, I like the sight of his bare chest. He is a far larger man than any of my handlers. In fact, my Rhodes is even larger than Killian, but without the puffy aspects.

"You got it," says my Rhodes. With a wink in my direction, he marches off to the back of the bus. I suppose he stores clothing there under his bunk.

Rhodes is no sooner gone than Chase You Dick slips onto the empty seat beside me. This is unfortunate, especially considering how Chase You Dick has his guitar with him.

"Was I unclear?" I ask. "I do not like you or your playing."

Chase You Dick grabs his heart in a show of pretend sorrow. "Don't say that, kitten."

"I am not a kitten."

"You're a beautiful girl."

"Neither am I a girl." I tilt my head and think this through. "If this display is because you wonder if I am interested in you, then the answer is *no*. You treated Shawna in a shoddy way, Chase You Dick. We *women* notice these things."

Fresh laughter erupts from around the bus. Strange what this band finds as funny.

Chase You Dick hoists his guitar onto his lap. "Give me a chance," he says. "Let me play a little. I bet I'll change your mind."

"No."

But Chase You Dick does not seem to understand the word 'no.' He begins to play anyway. "This is one that Kaps wrote," he says. "It's called, *Pretty*."

I lean back into my seat. *Pretty?* That could be a nice song. And if I'm being honest, I do love any kind of music. I shall listen to Chase You Dick. Sadly, he has a whiny voice which does not improve as he begins to sing.

I'm so pretty
Young and witty
Yeah!
I got lots of money
Kiss me honey
Yeah!

Wow.

What a terrible song.

My Rhodes settles into the chair across from mine at the table. He makes a silly face every time the song goes, *Yeah!* I can't help but grin.

Chase You Dick finishes the tune and catches how I smile. He gets the wrong idea, of course, and believes that I enjoy his playing. And now that my Rhodes is here? I do like the performance in a way.

So Chase Your Dick keeps singing terrible stuff while my Rhodes and I make silly faces at each other. Mostly, we pretend different ways of offing ourselves in time to the music. It is fun. I'd forgotten the joy of goofing around with another. It is certainly something I never did with my handlers.

Hours pass before Nikki pulls into our camp site. Chase You Dick leans in. "What do you say, Ves? Want to share my tent?"

I roll my eyes. This is ridiculous. Since basic words like 'yes' and 'no' do not work with this fellow, I rise, stand on the table, and jump off into the aisle. Then I turn to my Rhodes. "Are you ready? I should like to share a tent with you."

My Rhodes is laughing so hard, he can only nod in reply. Together, we head off the bus and to what the others call a campground.

It looks nothing like a cave.

A small fire crackles in the center of a clearing. All around, people set up tents like the ones I saw at Trance-a-dance. Nikki fires up some burgers which are even more delicious than the ones I ate at the Lone Star Diner. It is nice to share time with a group, but at the same time, I can't stop thinking about the ceremony on Friday.

Killian admitted to killing Gracie. When my lead handler opened Pandora's box, it upset my Rhodes so much, he almost electrocuted the countryside. No doubt, Killian has hurt my Rhodes as well.

As I finish my third burger, I come to a decision. If anyone can help me understand my vow with Killian, it will be my Rhodes. And certainly, my Rhodes has been trying to help me. The truth is, I have been holding back.

Well, only five days remain before Friday. I do not have time to wait before I trust my Rhodes with my secrets. I must take a chance and tell him more.

My Rhodes sits beside me on a felled log. He holds a stick in his hands which he pokes into the fire.

"Psst," I whisper.

My Rhodes leans in. "What is it, Ves?"

"May we go for a walk?" I ask. "I would like to speak with you."

Chase You Dick stands. "You guys going for a hike? Let me join you."

My Rhodes leans in. "Let's go back to the bus," he says in a low voice. "There are enchantment spells on it to keep the noise inside and intruders out. We can talk there."

"That would be good." I rise. "My Rhodes and I are going to the bus." I stare at Chase You Dick. "We should like to be alone."

Everyone starts whistling and laughing. "She got you there," says the man with the mask.

"Friend zone," adds Bash of the Drummer Men. After that, both band members throw bits of paper at Chase You Dick. They really are strange, these men and the things they find hilarious.

My Rhodes stands and takes my hand. Together, we head back to the bus. Other campfires crackle off through the trees. We are not the only ones here. Crickets sound in the undergrowth. A green scent mixes with the charcoal and flame. Overhead, the night sky shows far fewer stars than in the desert. That is a pity.

My Rhodes unlocks the bus and we step inside. I am anxious to begin our talk, so I slide into the first set of seats up front. My Rhodes take a place beside me.

"What's up?" he asks.

"I wasn't telling you everything before. That must change."

My Rhodes nods. "I'm here."

"I spoke about a ceremony before. It takes place in five days. In it, I shall take on the power of a great dragon."

"Through Pandoras's box?" asks my Rhodes.

"That's right. How did you know?"

"Pandora's box is famous in the dragon lands. There are a lot of rumors about it, but no one really knows what it can do. *Taking on ghost powers* is one of its legends." My Rhodes takes in a long breath. "I think someone used Pandora's box when Father died. Titan—that's my father—was covered in the same little red dots that Killian used to disappear. I was, too."

I pop my hand over my mouth. "That is terrible."

"It is, but what's more important now is keeping you safe. I've heard Pandora's box recharges with the height of the starfall. Is that true?"

I nod. "That is when the ceremony takes place. Five days from now."

My Rhodes scrubs his hands over his face. "There's a bigger pattern here, but I can't see it yet. I have to admit, stuff that's related to the day Father died ... it messes with my mind." My Rhodes opens his mouth, as if to say more. Then he shakes his head and refocuses on me. "What else do you know about the ceremony? Can we find another dragon shifter to volunteer and take your place?"

"I do not know. I have spent many years training to take on these extra powers. It in unlikely we could find someone else in a matter of days."

"Maybe we capture Killian? Grill him for information?"

A chill rolls up my spine. I hug my elbows. "This is the challenge. There are many possibilities of what we could do. Yet it is hard to decide without my memory. I promised to follow through with the ceremony; my vow protects my family. Breaking that magical promise will have consequences. What if I do something that frees me from the ceremony, but it hurts my family?"

My Rhodes nods. "I understand. Give me a little time to think on it. There's something we can do, Ves. I won't lose you."

His words make me feel all squirmy inside. "May I ask *you* some questions now?"

"Sure."

"You fight well. Is that usual for guitar men?"

"No, my job is to protect the band. Usually."

"In the tent at Dance-a-trance there was a girl singer. Do you protect her, too?"

"I try. It isn't easy."

"That is shocking. You make it look so simple. Back when we were riding here, Chase sang many awful songs. But one tune used a word I like for you. Swagger."

My Rhodes raises his brows. "Meaning?"

"The way you walk. You can handle yourself."

My face heats. *How could I have been so silly?* Now he might know that I've been looking at him.

My Rhodes shifts on the chair. He is even closer now. I am keenly aware of every place our bodies touch. "What part of me has swagger exactly?" he asks.

"I don't remember." My face burns even hotter. I stare at the floor. Now my Rhodes definitely knows I've been looking at him.

My Rhodes runs his finger along my jawline. With gentle movements, he guides my gaze to meet his. "I like how you look at me, Ves."

That urge returns. The one where I want to press our mouths together. What is the word? Kiss. That's it. I keep staring at his lips. What would it be like?

"You…" I stammer. "You're…" This is so awful. Just kiss him. I am a warrior, after all. How can I be afraid of a little kiss?

My Rhodes must be thinking the same thing. We move in unison, closing the space between us.

"Rhodes, are you there?" It is a woman speaking. How strange. Her tone is familiar and not, all at the same time. "Will you accept our communication? It's urgent."

"Damn." My Rhodes stands. "Stay here, Ves. I must talk with someone."

"Talk? I thought we were alone."

"We are. It's a magical video call."

"Video." This gets more confusing by the second.

"Basically, I need to talk to some people as ghosts."

"Ah. That makes sense." Gracie taught me about spells that separate your astral body in order to go places and do things. My Rhodes is important. It makes sense that people would be summoning him. "I shall wait here."

"Great," says my Rhodes. "I'll be right back."

As he strides away, I keep thinking about the woman's voice I heard before.

Rhodes, are you there?

It triggers something inside me. My inner crystal ball flares to life once more. This lady is important, I know it.

I just do not remember.

27

RHODES

*L*eaving Ves at the front of the bus, I slip into my regular spot at the tables. A ghostly version of Portia and Tempest are waiting for me.

"I'll take the communication," I state.

Portia blinks. "There you are." Now that I've accepted her spell, we can see each other. She'll only see me and whoever is right beside me; that's how the spell works. Ves will stay hidden from view, which is a good thing. If Ves enters the picture, that will raise more questions than I can answer right now.

"We are so worried," says Portia. "There are rumors about. Disturbing ones."

"What have you heard?" I ask.

"Killian has Pandora's box," states Tempest.

I nod. "He does."

Portia gasps. "How do you know?"

"Trust me; I know." There's no way I'm getting into a conversation about Ves and the ceremony right now. Best to keep things high level.

"We confronted Killian about it," adds Tempest. "But he has some story about a counterfeit box that carried some old spells."

Tempest leans forward. "I know you, mate. You don't want to tell us lots of details. But this is important. How do you know about Killian and Pandora's box?"

"I ran into Killian on the road," I explain. "He did have something that looked like Pandora's box. And yes, it carried barely any magic. In fact, I think he used up whatever was in there."

Portia eyes me carefully. "So in your opinion, it was a fake?"

How I wish I could avoid this answer. I loathe the idea of putting Ves at risk, but here are my emperor and empress. They deserve the truth. "No, I think it was the real thing. Pandora's box will recharge at the height of Pandora's starfall."

"In that case, the situation is even more serious," says Tempest. He and Portia share a long look before continuing. "We've gotten word about a ceremony that will take place at the height of Pandora's starfall. It will raise the spirit of Chimera."

Pure shock jolts my nervous system. Ves told me about taking on powers at the ceremony. *Could that be Chimera?*

"Are you all right?" asks Portia.

"I'll deal," I reply. "The Chimera news comes as a surprise, that's all."

"It's not my favorite, either," says Tempest. "Listen to me carefully. This ceremony of Pandora's box is supposed to give someone the magic of a past spirit. But I know my father. If his energy gets into someone, he'll take them over entirely. We'll have another Chimera on our hands, only one who is even more powerful than before."

I rub my temples, trying to process this information. "What do you need me to do?"

"Make sure Kaps is here on Friday. Her birthday will be celebrated dinner, but the afterwards we're holding a public concert."

I pull on my ear lobe. I must have heard that wrong. "Concert?"

"Didn't Kaps tell you?" asks Portia. "She and Huntress contacted us yesterday. Kaps informed us about the big concert in Furonium with Cool Daze. It will be free and open to everyone."

"Kaps didn't tell me in so many words." I let out a frustrated huff of breath. "But she made it known that she had something big planned to make a point. It's just ..." I rake my fingers through my hair.

"What aren't you telling us?" asks Portia.

"It's like this," I say. "Kaps is just ... Kaps. I wouldn't invite the whole kingdom."

"We didn't, mate," says Tempest. "Kaps already did."

"And it could be for the best," adds Portia. "The people love Kaps. If this concert goes wrong, it will help everyone understand why she might need to go away for a while."

"Meaning the tower," I say.

"I'm not talking about the royal dungeons," says Portia. "The tower complex has a library, a gym ... every convenience you can imagine. It's just safer for her."

"Why not take her now?" I ask.

Tempest and Portia share another long look. "We've been trying for weeks," says Portia. "You know how Kaps is. She can lose any guard, except for you and Huntress."

A sickly feeling settles into my stomach. "I won't ambush her and drag her in."

"We aren't asking you to, mate." Tempest's gaze turns intense. "Just get her here by Friday. We'll do the rest."

"Hopefully, everything will be fine," adds Portia hopefully. "But the minute anything looks off, we'll have extra guards on duty, including your uncle Atlas."

Translation? If Kaps makes one false move on Friday, then she's in the tower. And honestly? It's in Kaps' nature to make false moves. The princess is totally ending up in the tower on Friday. It's just a question of the hour they turn the key.

"Do you understand?" asks Tempest.

"I get it." *And I do.* It's amazing Tempest and Portia have been this patient with Kaps. But with Pandora's box out there? They simply must crack down. If they can't find Kaps on the road, then Friday is the day. "I'll see Kaps tomorrow night the show in San Antonio. I'll reach out to you both if anything seems off."

A scent fills the air. Peach blossoms and sunshine. Ves is near. "Look," I say to Portia and Tempest. "I've got to run. I'll be in touch."

"Please," says Portia.

With that, their ghostly images disappear. The magical communication is over.

Turning around, I find Ves standing in the aisle behind me. Her face is pale with shock. "Who were those people?"

"Our emperor and empress."

"Ah." Ves turns and speeds away. As she marches off, she calls over her shoulder. "I shall take my dragon form now." With that, she rushes off the bus, transforms into a great gray beast and takes to the skies.

I shift and fly after her. Losing Ves? Still not going to happen.

ZINNIA

*a*s I soar over the human forest, my mind is a jumble. The image of the crystal ball keeps overwhelming my mind's eye. In it, I see glimpses of the man and woman that my Rhodes spoke with.

Who were those people?

As I fly along, more pictures appear in my head. There's a golden palace. Red seas. A great line of black mountains. It's my past, I know it.

A headache bites into my temples. This is like what happens when I read my little book, only far worse.

Air currents shift across my scales. Looking over, I see a great green dragon flying at my side.

My Rhodes.

The forest opens up into a small stretch of grass. The area looks deserted. I take in a breath. The place smells also devoid of anything but animals. The headache spikes down my neck.

I can't keep flying.

Time to set down.

Arching my wings, I land onto the open space. My great dragon claws slice through the wet grass. I transform into my human shape once more and immediately regret it. The night is cold.

An electric charge fills the air. *Magic.* It must be my Rhodes. A blanket gets wrapped around my shoulders. Turning, I see my Rhodes framed by the moonlight. I can only see his barest outline in the darkness.

"You know magic," I say. "You conjured a covering and placed it on me."

"I know a little magic. I'm only half dragon. My powers aren't as great as some others." He pulls me against his chest. His skin is bare and the blanket is between us. Still, it is the closest embrace that I have ever experienced.

"What happened back there?" he asks.

The words tumble from my mouth. "I recognized them."

"That's our emperor and empress. Everyone in Furonium has seen their picture many times."

"While they were talking, I got visions. More hit me after I flew away. There were black mountains and a crimson sea."

"That's Furonium. You've been there, Ves. There must have been a time before the cave when you were a regular Furor."

"My handlers told me I was the last of the Furor. For years, I worked to be prepare my soul as a vessel for another spirit. That's the ceremony."

"I've heard how Pandora's box can make your body house another spirit. What ghost will take yours?"

"Chimera."

My Rhodes sighs. "Oh, Ves."

"I shall only take Chimera's powers, and then only to repair the Furor world."

He cups my face in his hands. "Listen to me carefully, Ves. Chimera is evil. If he wants to repair the world, it's only to wipe out people like me. Part humans. They call us scrubs."

"No." A sick taste enters my mouth. "I'm supposed to save people. Killian never said anything about scrubs."

"I know this is hard for you, but you must hear it. That ghostly man you saw? That's Tempest. He said Chimera's soul would take over whoever it touched. It wouldn't be taking on powers, Ves. It would be erasing *you*."

Fresh flashes appear in the crystal ball. There's an old man ... Oswine ... he took in Chimera's soul and changed into something evil. In the blink of an eye, the vision is gone.

I pull the blanket more tightly around me. "Perhaps I could still take in the ghost's power. Maybe I can use it against people like Killian."

"You spoke about a vow before. Something about your past."

"Yes, I made a magical promise to protect my family. A spell binds my memories into a crystal ball."

"Crystal ball." My Rhodes looks away, his gaze lost in thought. "There are royal mages who specialize in these things." My Rhodes focuses on me once more. "Come with me to Furonium. We'll find a way to get your memory spell broken."

"Must it be Furonium?"

"That's where the best mages are. One of them may be able to break a crystal ball spell. And as you said, you need your memory back before you can do anything else. It makes sense, Ves. You can't make changes that hurt your family."

The chill of the night seems to enter my very bones. "I don't know if I could go to the dragon lands. I only saw a new face a few days ago." The very thought of Furonium makes my knees wobble. "I shall consider it; is that acceptable?"

"It's a start." My Rhodes pulls me close once more. "You're shivering."

"That is odd. I am no longer cold."

"Maybe I know why." My Rhodes leans in. His breath cascades down my neck. My heart flutters while he speaks in a low whisper. "I feel connected to you."

Before, being around my Rhodes helped me feel safe. Now, that changes. Lines of something wind between me and my

Rhodes. I loop my arms around him and tighten our embrace. There is so much I want to say, yet I can't seem to find the words.

Leaning back, I stare at my Rhodes in the moonlight. He is too handsome to be real.

And that's when I notice it.

My tail cuff now flares with red light.

My Rhodes steps away. He sees the same thing. "I knew it. They're using your tail cuff to track you. We need to get out of here."

I straighten my shoulders. We do need to run off, but not before I do one simple thing. Going up on tiptoe, I brush my lips across my Rhodes' cheek. Magic flares up around us. And electric sense fills the air.

Snap!

My tail cuff breaks in two. My tail transforms from gray to black. For a long moment, my Rhodes and I simply stare at the broken spell.

"You're Firelord tribe, not Thorntail," whispers my Rhodes.

"What does that mean?"

"He stole you from a Firelord family to put you in his training program and big ceremony. It makes sense; Thorntails are not the best warriors."

"So my family is Firelord." I turn the idea over in my mind. It does feel right.

"It's a massive tribe. It will take time to find your family, but it's possible." His green eyes are filled with sadness. I know what he is thinking. If my true scales had been discovered years ago, my family might have been located. But now? There is simply not enough time.

That when the scent of vinegar carries on the air.

Killian is near. And my handlers are with him.

No question what to do next. Without another word, my Rhodes and I take our dragon forms and soar away.

29

RHODES

*V*es and I fly back to the campgrounds. Once there, we realize our big error: we never set up a tent. So we wing our way back to the bus. It's more private, too.

Once we land, Ves and I shift back to our human forms. I'd conjure up more blankets for us, but it's pitch dark by the bus. I can't see my hand in front of my face, let alone anything interesting on Ves. I fumble around in the dark until I find the bus' door. It's still open. Ves asks to wait outside, so I climb into the bus and grab myself a pair of sleep pants.

Since I'm now an expert at rifling through Kaps' drawers, I grab some sleep pants and a T-shirt for Ves. I leave the stuff at the front of the bus and flick the lights on and off. That's our signal; it's all right to come in. While Ves enters, I take the chance to hit the mini bathroom. It's been a big day, so I figure we can both use a little privacy.

By the time I get out, Ves has already climbed into her—and that means it used to be my—old bunk. I peek through the curtains. Ves is totally asleep. I slide into one of the empty bunks we use for the occasional roadie. I can never sleep on the bus, so I don't expect to rest.

Yet I fall right asleep.

At some point during the night, I dream that Ves slips into my bunk. Then I wake up.

Hold on.

Ves really *is* in my bunk.

We're lined up like a pair of spoons in a drawer. It's a tight squeeze, but I wouldn't have it any other way. I spend far too much time watching her shoulders rise and fall. This might be the most exciting night of my life.

I might never fall asleep again.

But I do anyway.

While I'm resting, I dream that Ves sings in her sleep. She whispers words that sound like a music. I cuddle in closer and listen.

Ves is singing *Our Song*, the very tune I wrote with Zin. There's no way Ves could know the words, though. I never sang when I played it at Trance-a-Dance.

Must be a dream.

Yes, that's it.

I've been gifted a night of holding Ves while I dream she's sings new words to *Our Song*.

Hard to imagine anything better.

30

ZINNIA

I wake up with one thought on my mind.

Four days until the ceremony.

And yes, I might also be thinking that it's nice to be held by my Rhodes. Which its most definitely true.

Yet it is hard to enjoy such things when there is a big decision to be made. Namely, I must decide whether to visit Furonium.

Logically, it makes a lot of sense to enter the dragon realms. I can not approach Killian for help. And my Rhodes has carefully considered what he can do to assist. Visiting the mages of Furonium is his best idea.

Even so, every time I consider accepting this offer, my head aches so much, I fear that it might split open. That horrible red crystal ball keeps appearing in my mind. The orb flares barrage of images that vanish too quickly for me to process.

All in all, I fear that my Rhodes is right. I did have a history in Furonium. And going there in person will tear my world open in ways I can not imagine.

What if my family are horrible people?

How do I know I wasn't raised to worship Chimera?

There must be some reason why my head burns in agony every time I consider the visit.

So I decide to think about other things.

While we have breakfast, I try to contemplate a good formal name for the guitar player with a mask. I come up empty.

When my Rhodes asks me if I am all right, I insist that I am still sleepy and hide out in my bunk. There, I consider ways that I might fight Killian. This is more soothing than the naming exercise.

Next I consider how many burgers is enough for a meal while we have lunch at another diner.

Afterward, I once again pretend to need a nap afterwards. My Rhodes knows that I am avoiding him, but he doesn't press me. It is a good thing, too. Every nerve in my body is like a spring that's coiled too tightly.

How can I decide to visit Furonium?

Why would I choose to do anything else?

At last, we arrive at the site of the band's performance. It is another outdoor festival. Unlike Dance-a-trance, each stage is contained within its own circus-style tent, complete with an arched roof.

My Rhodes gets busy setting up the stage. Watching him work is like standing beside a bright sign that reads, *make your choice!*

More and more, I know I can not visit Furonium. Perhaps it is magic that keeps me away. If so, then I would need a stronger counter-spell to find the strength to go.

It is hard to imagine anything that would be that potent.

While my Rhodes and the band set up their stage, I wander through the festival itself. There are many tables with handmade things. I find another human who sells T-shirts from a blanket, only hers read, *San Antonio Music Fest.* It is puzzling how humans make such different clothing and yet do not use magic.

Mortals are rather clever that way.

I also find a row of miniature metal wagons that offer various foods. The smells are delicious. I decide that I would like to try French fries and funnel cakes. However, none of the sellers have demons on them, so I must locate human money with which to buy things.

I'm about to find Nikki and ask her for some gold when Chase You Dick steps out of the shadows.

"Hey, Ves."

"Hello, Chase You Dick."

"I heard you humming before," he says.

"Was I humming? I did not realize that fact."

"Yes, I recognized the rune. It was *Worship Me*, one of the songs I played for you on the bus."

"Ah." I have perfect memory, which is why I can't get that awful tune out of my ahead. Not that I'll share this fact right now.

"What do you mean, *ah*?" Chase You Dick bobs his eyebrows.

"Is there something wrong with your face?" I point to his brows. "Your head fur is acting strangely."

"Head fur? Oh, my eyebrows. I'm fine. Just wondering why you said *ah*."

This is now the stupidest conversation I've ever had.

"I said 'ah' because I do not know what else to say. I hum, it is true. And I am not interested in you romantically. I feel like we keep re-hashing the same conversation."

Chase You Dick laughs and that's when I scent it. *Alcohol.* He reeks. "You should not be drinking," I state.

"I'm of age. It's just a little fun."

"You are walking around while drinking alone. How is that fun?"

"I'm not alone. I have you." To emphasize that point, Chase You Dick tries to pull me into his arms. At the same time, he opens his mouth to expose a very pointy tongue. I suppose he wishes to kiss me. The thought makes me ill, so I order my tail to loop about his ankle and pull.

Whump.

Chase You Dick falls onto his back with a satisfying thud. Stepping over his prone form, I head toward the preparation tent for the band.

Interacting with Chase You Dick was incredibly annoying. It should have fully taken my mind off my major decision about visiting Furonium.

Only it did not. And that is worrisome indeed.

RHODES

I wait by the entrance to our dressing tent, watching the crowd for any sign of Kaps. We're on in five minutes and she still hasn't shown.

Even for Kaps, this is cutting it close.

Inside the tent, it's a familiar scene. Only instead of bean bags, the band now hangs out on folding chairs. Livingston paces the floor while wearing his ghost mask. Bash plays drums on an empty trash can. And Chase is even awake. How did that ever happen?

Although, to be honest, I have my ideas. Ves sits apart from the others. Chase keeps rubbing a huge bump on the back of his head while glaring at Ves. My guess is that our lead drinker tried to hit on Ves and got flattened. Literally.

Serves him right.

I check my watch. *Four minutes.*

Damn. This gig isn't like the Dance-a-trance. We can't switch times or anything. We hit the stage or leave on the bus.

Bash acts as the *chilly voice of reason* here. "Make the call, Rhodes." There's no question what he means. *We need to cancel.*

I keep scanning the crowd. Still no sign of Kaps. "She'll be here. She always shows."

"Maybe," says Livingston. "But she's been cutting it closer and closer lately. We should think of other alternatives."

This ought to be good. "Meaning?"

"Livingston and I have been talking," says Chase. "Why don't we teach Kaps a little lesson?" He points to Ves. "Let's make the *nut job dragon* sing in her place."

My mouth falls open with surprise. *Ves? Sing?*

"You have to admit it," says Livingston. "It's a great idea. And our red flag fan can totally do it. She already knows the words to every song. And we all wear masks anyway. It will be fine."

Bash stops drumming on the trash bin. "Actually, that's a good idea."

"Of course it is," says Livingston. "And we did not haul ourselves here just to miss the gig when we have a perfectly good replacement."

I raise my hands with my palms forward. It's the universal symbol for, *stop right there.* "We are not forcing Ves to do anything."

Ves rises from her chair. "You will not force me. I wish to do this."

I step closer to Ves. She's been quiet all day, avoiding conversation and staring off into space. I get it. She has some big decisions to make. I've been trying to give her some space.

"Are you sure?" I ask.

"Yes, I remember all the words. And who knows what will happen tomorrow? I should like to sing now." A desperate gleam shines in Ves's eyes. She needs this. A distraction.

"All right," I say. "If you're ready."

But Livingston is already handing out chicken masks. Ves refuses, putting on the some sunglasses instead. Which makes sense. Kaps wears wigs all the time, so Ves' eyes are the only thing that will stand out.

And with that, it's official.

This has all the makings of a disaster.

RHODES

*T*he band and I march through the crowd. Our destination? The performance tent for our gig. As we move along, I can't help but notice how all the other bands are playing country and western stuff. Not that I don't like that kind of music myself.

It's just that Cool Daze doesn't play anything similar. At all.

Soon we reach our tent. Security lets us in through the back. The band gets up on stage; their gear is set and ready to go. The inside of the tent is a little smaller than our space at Dance-a-trance. Plus, there's no sound board. That said, someone did put out a bowl of Cheesy Doodles on a table in back. A few teenagers hang out at that spot.

Sad.

If we didn't have free Cheesy Doodles, we wouldn't even have those two in here.

Why did Kaps book this gig again? No doubt, it had more to do with finding some kind of Furor treasure in Texas rather than a performance that actually made sense.

That's Kaps for you.

I stand by the Cheesy Doodle kids and keep watch for danger.

Meanwhile, the band grabs their equipment, setting off a chorus of thuds and screeching noises. Did I mention there's no sound board in here? There isn't. Just our instruments and some small speakers we drag along for emergencies. The Cheesy Doodle kids wince and cover their ears. If they still didn't have a half-bowl of snacks left, they would definitely have run off.

In short order, the band is all in place. Bash on drums. Chase on lead guitar. Livingston and his bass. Ves at the microphone. A pang of longing moves through my soul. For the first time in ages, I actually ache to perform.

Ves and I share a long look. I give her an encouraging nod. There are no words between us. Even so, I hope the meaning is clear.

You can do this.

Ves sighs, strolls over to Chase, and whispers something to him. They chatter back and forth for a bit. My warrior sense goes on alert. Did Chase do something to upset Ves?

Turns out, the opposite is true. Chase's face melts into a pout that would make a two-year old proud. He peels off his guitar, stares at me, and holds the instrument out in my direction.

I don't need to be asked twice.

Of course, I'm playing.

I race up to the stage and take Chase's instrument from his hands. His face is still in full-on toddler pout. "She won't play unless you're here," whines Chase.

"Better than missing the gig, right?" I ask.

"Whatever," snarls Chase. "I'm finding the beer tent." With that, he marches off stage with maximum drama. And by that, I mean he does not exit through the access flap behind the stage. Nope. Chase does a full prima donna stroll across the empty audience floor, followed by a dramatic pause by the front entrance flap. After flipping us the bird, Chase storms off into the festival.

The Cheesy Doodle kids watch the whole scene in fascination. By now, both have orange halos around their mouths. It kinds works considering how Bash and Livingston are wearing chicken masks.

My life is so strange.

With Chase gone, I turn to Ves. "What do you want to start off with?"

"I'd like to kick off with *Goodbye Sunshine*," she replies. We all nod. Ves then gives us the full set list. She scans each of our faces in turn. "What do you think? Is that an acceptable series of songs?"

"Wait, was that an actual set list?" asks Livingston.

"I think that was a set list," adds Bash.

"Works for me." I nod to Ves. "We're good to go."

"One sec," calls Bash. "It's too hot in here."

Seeing how Ves and I aren't wearing our masks, Bash now pulls off his as well. There's no point asking Livingston whether he wants to remove his.

"I'll start singing with Rhodes on lead guitar," declares Ves. "Then you guys drop in when you feel it. So you know, I plan to do the songs differently."

Huh. How can we do the songs any more differently than we do now? We've never played the same tune in the same way twice. That said, we're all very used to trying to follow along with our lead singer.

"We're good," I tell Ves.

Nodding, Ves turns to the microphone. "Good afternoon. We're Cool Daze and this first tune is called *Goodbye Sunshine*."

This is another *first* for us: An introduction of the band that actually gives our name and the first song. Normally Kaps talks about whatever she's into that day. Mostly, it's Furor artifacts. Not exactly a crowd pleaser.

Ves then launches into the lyrics a cappella. Her voice starts off as husky and low.

Find me a path
That doesn't lead to you
Give me a time
Not better spent with you
Your smile is my life
Your dreams are my own
I leave it all for you
Our thread fully sewn

Usually this song is another one of Kaps' scream fests. The band plays along, fast and loud. But today, Ves slows the tune into a lovely ballad. I cut in with a gentle counter rhythm until Ves launches into the big refrain.

Goodbye sunshine
Farewell stars
Forsake the future
Forget the scars
I follow you
We share the night
We birth a true love
Our heart's delight

I get lost in the music. All too soon, the song is done. An amazing sight greets me afterwards.

We have an audience.

About a dozen humans stand in the back of the tent. The Cheesy Doodle bowl is empty, so they can't be here for the free food.

It's Ves. She attracted actual listeners here.

We segue to the next tune. Each time, the band follow the same steps. Ves and I kick things off, then the rest of the group joins in. All our screechy songs turn into something slow and lovely. It's a totally different vibe, but the way the tent fills with people? It's also an actual hit, so no complaints here. Some mortals even pull out their cell phones to record things. That's new.

As each tune passes, this situation becomes more and more surreal. Bands play for years to find their sound. How could Ves and I find ours so quickly?

An hour flies by before I see her. *Kaps.*

The princess pulls a reverse-Chase drama maneuver. She whips the tent flap open and stands in the entrance. Rays from the setting sun highlight her from behind. Kaps waits there, scans the tent, and then marches up on stage. Ves is in the middle of a song.

Ves stops singing.

The band falls silent.

Our audience merely stares at the whole scene, stunned. Not that I blame them. People just don't walk onstage during shows like this.

Kaps points to the microphone. The statement is clear if unspoken. *Hand it over.*

Nodding, Ves steps away. Moving in, Kaps grabs the mic. "Thanks for listening to hear Cool Daze! Have a great night Houston!"

"We're in San Antonio," I say, but Kaps doesn't hear me. She marches off stage and exits through the back flap.

Once again, the meaning is clear. *Follow me.*

As I watch Kaps leave, I shake my head in disbelief.

What a Kaps thing to do.

ZINNIA

The band and I return to the preparation tent, which is a shame. Singing with Rhodes was such a joy. Then Kaps shows up and ends it all. She's the very singer I had to replace.

I think back to when I first met Kaps. What did she call me again?

Creepy.

That settles things. I do not like Kaps, and is not simply because she calls me names or cuts my show short. No, it is more the way Kaps now drags Rhodes into a corner and whispers in his ear. All the while, Kaps keeps blinking up at my Rhodes and finding reasons to touch him. With each passing second, fresh fire burns in my veins.

This is my Rhodes.

Not hers.

Some dusty corner of my brain screams that I should focus on something else. Namely, I need to let Rhodes know I have made my decision.

I shall never visit Furonium.

All that remains is breaking the news to my Rhodes. This is a big undertaking. I should be deciding how to approach him, not focusing on the way Kaps blinks in his direction.

Yet her blinking is maddening. It makes me want to poke her in the eyes.

Or trip her with my tail.

Perhaps both.

Try as I might, I cannot think of anything outside of my Rhodes and Kaps. Every instinct I have tells me that this Kaps is somehow using my Rhodes. Hurting him. And yes, drawing away his affection.

That must end.

RHODES

*I*t was bad enough that Kaps rushed us offstage. Now, she's pulled me into a corner of the prep tent for a one-on-one.

I really need a new job.

Kaps links her fingers with mine. "You won't believe this."

I pointedly separate my hands from hers. "Go on."

"I almost got Pandora's box. As in, *the* Pandora's box! Or technically, L'Griffe almost took it. We both missed our target this time. You'll never guess who has it now."

"Hmm," I tap my chin. "Could it be Killian, the Master Dragon of the Thorntails?"

"Yeah, how did you guess? Killian's totally got Pandora's box. There were rumors before, but now I know for a fact that it's totally true. Killian's been flashing the container around for months now, bragging what it can do. He even cast a few spells in public. That's what got L'Griffe interested. We got so close to cornering him."

"And now?" I ask. On reflex, I shoot another glance in Ves' direction. She stands across the tent, pretending not to notice me and Kaps.

This is not good.

"Killian vanished," answers Kaps. "Huntress is tracking him down right now." Pausing, Kaps eyes me carefully. "How does this affect the Furor Girl? You keep staring at her while we talk about Pandora's box."

"Why would it effect her?"

"Come on, we both know it does. Just spill."

I don't like the idea of betraying Ves's trust, but I do need Kaps to share her mages with us. It's best to use the truth. "Killian plans to use Pandora's box to channel a soul into Ves."

Kaps checks her manicure. "Wow. That sucks for Ves."

Protective energy courses up my back. "You don't seem too broken up."

"Well, it's like this. Ves will get extra dragon powers, right?"

Now, I've gotten similar speeches from Kaps. They all start with, *well, it's like this.* She's scheming again. Not that she ever stopped in the first place.

"What are you up to?" I ask.

"The new girl did a good job on stage, that's all."

"Kaps." I lower my voice. "Where is this going?"

"I know where Pandora's box has gone; I *will* find it. All I need are two more days, tops. The big celebration is in three days. Friday. Huntress is already on the trail. I just stopped by to let you know our plans. Once I have Pandora's box, I'll mosey on over to Furonium. There's plenty of time. No problem."

I fight the urge to groan. "After this gig, the tour is over. You're supposed to return directly to the palace for a family dinner and concert that *you* scheduled."

"And I will be there. But before we actually sit down and eat, people will only see me roaming the hallways and stuff. I *must* find Pandora's box. All I need is for someone who *looks like me* to show up and slink around."

At last, I see the scheme here. I fold my arms over my chest. "That's not Ves."

"Come on," counters Kaps. "This girl is wearing my clothes and singing my songs. And you're worried about this Killian casting spells to merge her with some other dragon?"

"I am."

"What better way to cure her than with Pandora's box? I will get it."

"That's not a lock and you know it." *That said, now's the time to segue to what I really want.* "But as princess, you *do* have the best palace mages around. Will they help Ves?"

"Sure! All of them totally love me. They're super loyal and discrete. They could cast tons of spells to help her."

I pinch the bridge of my nose. "I still don't like you going off. Your parents are serious about your safety, Kaps. If you don't show up on time, you're getting a one-way ticket to the tower."

Kaps rolls her eyes. "That space is a spa. Like I care."

"You will."

"Bah. Let them try and put me in a tower. Look, I'm going after Pandora's box anyway. You can help ... or get cut out of the loop."

I glance over at Ves. She only has three days left. And Kaps really has charmed the finest palace mages into serving her. Unless Ves pretends to be Kaps, it would take weeks of begging to get access to those mages. But if Ves were pretending to be the princess? Those mages will show up in a heartbeat. To break the spell on Ves' memory, this is the best shot.

I round on Kaps. "Two days. That's the most I can give you."

Kaps claps. "I will be there. Absolutely."

"Then go." I nod toward the exit. Kaps should take off before I change my mind.

"You're the best." Kaps kisses my cheek and speeds out of the tent. I look for Ves once more.

She's standing right beside me, and the look on her face makes my heart crumble. Ves saw that kiss.

Oh, no.

ZINNIA

Kaps was kissing my Rhodes. This is unacceptable.

My Rhodes says something about going to a palace and talking to mages. I nod and pretend to look interested. All my thoughts are on one concept.

I want to fight Kaps. She is after my Rhodes. That must not stand.

Once again, a small voice in the back of my mind screams that there is something important about Furonium which I must discuss with my Rhodes. Essentially, I can not visit any palace. I must stay here.

Yet I set those thoughts aside and focus on a different opportunity.

"So," I begin. "You believe I should visit a palace in Furonium and pretend to be Kaps."

"What do you think? I know it's a little out there, but you don't have much time."

"Will I see her chambers?" I ask.

My Rhodes tilts his head. "You'll have to. It's the only way to pretend to be her."

This is good news. Gracie always taught me to study my

enemy. Understanding motivation is the key to defeating anyone. And Kaps shall not win over my Rhodes.

I lift my chin. "In that case, I should be happy to visit the palace and play the princess. It will be enjoyable for me."

"Wow." My Rhodes takes a half-step backward. "I thought you'd fight me on this."

"Oh, no," I say with a grin. "I wish to be healed in Furonium."

And yes, I also want to scope out the enemy for the affection of my Rhodes as well.

Let this new battle begin.

ZINNIA

*W*e must wait until the morning to fly to Furonium. Rhodes tells me that there are certain clouds which only *appear* white and fluffy to humans. But to those of us who wield magic? We can detect a different haze about the edges. This is how we shall find a portal to the dragon lands.

Detect the right cloud.

Fly through.

Reach Furonium.

Only, like everything that has to do with magic, it is not easy. There are many different places in the after-realms. If we are not careful, we may end up inside a cloud that takes us to Hell or the Dark Lands. Neither sound enjoyable.

There are also portals under the ocean, but I am not a seafaring dragon like my Rhodes. I would drown before I found any such an access point.

And traveling by air is tricky. Turns out, one must fly during daylight hours in order to choose the right cloud.

All of which brings me to the present moment. We rested on the bus after the performance in San Antonio. A new morning is here. Now my Rhodes and I stand on the top of the metal wagon.

Three days remain before the great ceremony. The very thought makes me shiver. What will happen to me if I take in the spirit of Chimera? What fate will befall those I love if I do not?

It is time for answers.

Looking up to the sky, I pull my blanket more tightly around my shoulders. For his part, my Rhodes wears the SpongeBob towel about his waist. This way, we can shift without ruining any human clothing. Although I am suspicious of Kaps, I do not wish to destroy her wardrobe. And my Rhodes says it is easy to shred everything you own before you know what's happening.

So we wear a towel and a blanket.

I could say that it doesn't affect me to know we are a few scraps of fabric away from being naked with each other. But that would be a lie. Since my Rhodes' towel hangs low on his waist, I can not help but see the 'v' shape that points downward from his stomach. There is also a trail of dark hair there as well. It is fascinating.

"Are you ready?" asks my Rhodes.

I cough and look away. Did my Rhodes catch me staring? Probably. There is a knowing gleam in my Rhodes' green eyes. He *does* know I was looking at his body.

Yet I do not think he minds.

That makes everything even more complicated.

Clearing my throat, I force myself to focus on the task at hand. "I am ready," I state.

"On my mark," calls my Rhodes. "3… 2… 1!"

I leap up into the air while forcing my body to shift. Bits of white light shine beneath my skin as my flesh transforms into scales. Great wings spread behind me. I pump them in a steady rhythm and rise up into the clouds. Beside me, my Rhodes does the same.

Down below us, Nikki and Bates stand outside the bus.

"Don't get yourself killed!" warns Nikki. She is waving in the wrong direction. Poor mortals. Humans can not see our dragon forms. Bash points her to where we really are in the sky and Nikki shifts her wave in that direction.

"Be safe," calls Bash.

Together, my Rhodes and I soar through the skies. Wind streams across my scales. Sunlight warms my back. My Rhodes and I play off the airstream from each other, arcing and diving in an easy rhythm. It is like singing a song, only without music.

Hours pass as we search out the right cloud. All of them look similar to me, but my Rhodes will point out the magical ones. Mostly, this is so I can avoid them. As it happens, one tiny cloud goes to a place called Purgatory. While the Dark Lands and Hell do not seem interesting, I can not say the same for Purgatory. Something about that land calls my interest.

Ah, well. Something to contemplate later. That is, if I survive past Friday.

My Rhodes wheels onto his back so he flies upside down and beneath me. "The next cloud is the one."

I scan the nearby puffs of white. They all appear identical. *Which one counts as next?*

"I shall follow you, then," I say.

"Good idea."

My Rhodes then flips to fly right-side up once more. He speeds off into a nearby cloud and—POUF—he is gone. I push my wings to pump harder. All of a sudden, it strikes me that we've been flying for many hours. My home territory is rather small for dragons. Only twenty miles across. Endurance flying isn't something I have done before.

What if I am too slow?

Focusing all my energy, I speed to the place where my Rhodes vanished. For one moment, nothing surrounds me but a white haze. The next second? I soar over a red landscape. I take in a long breath.

Furonium.

A crimson sea rolls beneath me, ending in a beach made of

black sand. Once the beach ends, the ground becomes covered in a forest of tall trees with purple leaves. Those woods fade off into a great line of black mountains. A cascade of red lights arches over the lower peaks. *Pandora's starfall.* The tallest mountaintop is encircled with white clouds that glitter with gold. It is beyond lovely.

My Rhodes nods towards the golden clouds. "The palace is there."

I nod. My chest feels tight, like I can't pull in enough breath. The crystal ball image reappears in my mind. Pictures of the palace flash within its depths. A headache bites into my temples. The beat of my wings slows.

My Rhodes swoops so he flies below me once again. "Focus on me, Ves. Only me." He takes off at a greater speed.

I keep my gaze locked on my Rhodes. Pain burns through my arms and shoulders. My head turns fuzzy with the need for sleep. Things appear in my side vision, but I carefully keep my gaze locked on the great green dragon that is my Rhodes.

Even so, there is no missing the pay of light over the trees in the purple forest below. A blast of cool air hits me as we fly up the dark mountainside. Gold surrounds me when we reach the crown of clouds that surround the mountain's peak.

And then, past the golden clouds, a green vista opens below. There are a patchwork of fields and forests, of streams and roads. Little stone villages peep out through the canopy of trees. A massive golden palace is perched in the center of it all. The structure has turrets and windows. Mostly what I notice are the great balconies, though. Each one is large enough for a dragon to land upon.

"This way!' calls my Rhodes.

My eyes start to flutter shut on their own, but I force myself to stay close to my Rhodes. He arches his great green wings and lands on one of the lower balconies. I do the same.

The moment my claws land on stone, I shift back into my

human form. I vaguely notice a pink room with strange artwork. My Rhodes wraps a soft blanket around my shoulders and leads me to an impossibly large bed.

I climb atop the covers and fall instantly asleep.

I am here. Furonium.

RHODES

*V*es lays wrapped in the blanket I gave her. I make sure
the bedroom door is locked and then change into
some fresh clothes. Since I've snuck Kaps back into her room so
often, I have a cache of stuff here for just such occasions.

Once I'm in fresh jeans and a T, I go off to find one of my
contacts in the imperial kitchens. This is the fun part. Escape-
wise, Kaps picked out the best bedroom in the palace. It's easy to
hop off her balcony, scale down the palace walls, and then reach
the back larder for the kitchens.

In my experience, the back larder is the best place to secure
favors from servants.

Here's how it works. I complain a lot about having to follow
Kaps around, but the gig does have its advantages. Kaps is a pro
knowing *what* palace servants want *which* ancient trinkets in
exchange for favors. I'm not saying she bribes folks to help her
sneak around, but yeah.

She totally bribes servants all the time.

And since I'm Kaps' muscle, all I need to say is that Kaps is
back—in secret, of course—and how she needs a *fill in the
blank*. Sometimes it's food. Other cases, it's clothing. But what-

ever I am after, Kaps always needs it without her parents finding out.

That said, Tempest and Portia always discover the truth anyway. Eventually.

At this point, I figure I've got about twenty-four hours before the whole palace knows Ves and I are here. Until then, Kaps' secret network will keep us hidden.

After climbing down the palace exterior, I slip into the larder. Essentially, it's a small stone house where Cook stores things that need to stay dry, like flour. All of which means it's full of barrels which make perfect hiding spots to sit and wait. Most servants come through at least once a day.

Now some folks wonder why we don't use human technology in Furonium. That would be because we have magic. Why rewire a palace for electricity when you can just cast a spell? All of which is why the palace has a larder instead of a human-style fridge.

Back to my sneaking around.

I creep inside the small stone structure and hide behind a few barrels of flour. Then I wait, which gives me time to contemplate how this is me. Sitting in the dark. Doing crazy stuff for Kaps. Again.

Only this time, it's really for Ves, so the experience is far less humiliating. At least I've got that going for me.

Minutes pass before the door swings open and a lantern magically flares to life above. One of Cook's people comes in for some spices.

Good news. It's Helga.

I can tell this because I see a blue tail and there's only one snow dragon on the kitchen staff. Helga shuts the door. Time for me to swing into action. I step out from my hiding spot.

"Hey, Helga."

"Rho, is that you?" Helga steps closer. She's a sly creature with ice-blue eyes and short black hair. I'd guess her age to be in her late teens, although she carries herself like someone much older.

Helga's probably gotten more jewels out of Kaps than anyone else in the palace.

"It's me," I confirm. "Kaps is back. Can you send for the Zeta brothers?"

These guys are a trio of Hexenwing mages. Really good, too. Word is that the Zeta brothers are second only to the Mistress Dragon of their entire tribe. The Zetas also happen to be goofballs who spend a lot of time acting stupid with Kaps before getting to work. I'll have to think on how to shut that down. It's not like Ves has a ton of time here.

"Kaps has been away, right?" asks Helga slowly.

No question where this is going. "Sure."

"Did she bring anything back for me?"

Smart girl, that Helga. And these 'will you bribe me' conversations? They happen a lot. In fact, Kaps even set up a special *bribe drawer* for me in her chambers. The thing is loaded with what Kaps calls *Tier 3 Treasure* that I can use to buy people off as I see fit. What can I say? We have a system.

"Yeah," I reply. "There's a ruby pendant with your name on it."

"In that case, the brothers will be over in the morning."

I frown. "Why not now?"

"The palace is almost deserted. Most servants went home early because it's a such a big day tomorrow and Friday."

"Right. The ceremony."

"And you know the Zeta brothers. They bring a lot of drama. If we invite them in now, the guards will notice them for sure. Better to wait for the morning when the palace is a mob scene again."

I tilt my head and this think through. Helga is right. And this is why she'll probably retire early thanks to a personal jewel hoard from Princess Kappa. Helga is strategic. Ask her for something and it never goes wrong. That's worth cash money. Or in this case, one big-ass ruby.

We discuss a few more particulars—like Helga sneaking us in

some meals—and then the deal is done. After Helga takes off, I scale the wall once again to reach Kaps' room. This is one advantage of having an old-fashioned stone palace. Lots of handholds along the exterior wall.

Back in Kaps' room, I find Ves is still passed out. I drag a wooden armchair closer to the bed and try to sleep. Instead, I spend all night watching Ves. It's not too terrible. She's cute and makes little nose-snore noises.

It's late in the morning when a knock sounds on the door. I step over and whisper into the wood. "Who is it?"

"Zeta brothers."

"Give us a minute." I stroll over to the bed and tap Ves' shoulder. She awakens with a start.

"What? Who?" Ves clasps her blanket tightly around her shoulders.

"It's me, Rhodes." I take care to use my most soothing voice. "We're in Furonium. The mages are here to see you." I gesture towards Kaps' walk-in closet. "There are some clothes in there for you. You need to go in and get ready. Then the Zeta brothers will can examine what magic's been cast on you."

Ves blinks extra hard before speaking again. "So I can get rid of the crystal ball spell in my soul?"

"That's exactly right. Then you'll remember everything." *With any luck.*

Ves nods, yawns, and stumbles over to the walk-in closet. Once she's inside with the door closed, I let in the Zeta brothers and hope I've made the right decision.

Thing is, working with these three guys is like trying to nail Jell-O to a wall. Hard to make anything stick.

ZINNIA

I walk into a small room loaded with clothes. They are all piled onto shelves. Jammed along hangers. Or dangling from small bags that hook into the ceiling. It is more than a little overwhelming. Plus, there are more closet doors inside this first closet. I step up to the nearest one. A metal knob sits on the center panel along with a pointer. Around the dial are words like *heels*, *necklaces*, and *socks*.

This is too tempting.

I turn the dial to *heels* and open the door. Sure enough, the interior reveals another walk-in closet that is loaded with nothing but high-heeled shoes. I close the door and try again.

This time, I set the dial to *necklaces* and reopen.

Sure enough, the closet interior is now packed with glittery stuff of all shapes and kinds. Even more amazing, the walls hold shelves with stone busts. All the jewels are displayed on perfect replicas of Kaps' head and shoulders.

Being a princess is a serious undertaking.

I close the closet door and try to come up with a plan to find an outfit in here. Thankfully, Rhodes beat me to it. He has placed a yellow sundress on a chair, along with underthings and slippers. It is perfect. As I pull on my clothes, my pulse speeds.

Rhodes mentioned there were mages at the door. And not just any magic users, but the best of the best. These mages have been selected to care for a princess who needs enchanted closets to hold all her stuff.

Oh, my.

I spent years in the desert, trapped by Killian and my vow. All the while, my memories were stolen away. I still don't understand what could happen if I refuse to become the Vessel of the Future … assuming it is even possible for me to avoid this fate.

Taking in a deep breath, I grip the closet's handle. Outside this door stand the expert mages who may heal my mind and return my life. I push the door open.

In the center of Kaps' very pink room there stand three young men. All appear to be around Rhodes' age. Their tall frames are encased in black body leathers that are highlighted with feathers and jewels. Their dark green tails sway slowly behind them. Each wears a matching top hat. For whatever reason, I know where these mages come from.

Hexenwing tribe.

I shift my weight from foot to foot. These mages are a rather intimidating group.

"Hey, Kaps," they shout in unison. Then they move into an an acrobatic pose where one in the middle outstretches his arms to the side. With magical speed, the other two hop up to stand on the center man's arms. All three then stare at me with identical, almond-shaped eyes. In their collective opinion, one thing is clear: *I* am the one who is insane in this scenario.

"Come on, Kaps," says the one in the middle. "Don't leave us hanging. You're supposed to stand on my head."

I look.

Pause.

Think.

Look some more.

This is all very odd.

"Your head?" I ask.

Rhodes crosses the room to stand at my side. "I told you already, guys. Kaps got hit with a memory spell. She doesn't recall anything about the stuff you do."

"No high jinks?" asks the man on the left.

"No story time?" That's the center one talking. I do not know how he can be so casual while he has a fully-grown man standing on each arm.

"No tickle wars?" asks the one on the right.

I turn to my Rhodes. "Tickle wars? I thought these were serious mages."

"They are," explains my Rhodes. "It just takes them a little time to get organized." My Rhodes steps over and pulls on the tails of the far left and right men until they all stand on the floor once again.

"That is better," I say.

"You three need to start from the beginning. Give her your names."

"I'm Alpha Zeta," says the left one.

"I'm Beta Zeta," says the center.

"And I'm Eta Zeta," adds the right.

This is almost beyond belief. "Did you say Eta Zeta?"

"Yeah," says Eta. It seems they do not use formal greetings like I did back home. I shall try to adjust and only use first names instead of full ones. "Our parents won't win any awards for creativity."

Beta steps forward. "So, what seems to be the trouble?"

I take in a deep breath. *This is it.* "I can not recall anything. My memories are all trapped inside a red crystal ball."

"Memory wipe," says Beta.

"And related containment spell," adds Eta.

Alpha is the next one to step forward. "Let's talk about the real trouble here. What did you do to your hair? Why aren't you wearing any of the wigs we made for you?"

"It's a side affect of the memory spell," says my Rhodes quickly. "She found a magical artifact and—poof—her personal history is gone, along with her regular hairdo."

Now Eta steps up. Once more, the three men wait in a line. "And it changed your eye color, too. " Eta shakes his head. "It's so weird."

"Just another side affect," says Rhodes. "Now are you three going to conduct some tests and find out what's wrong?"

A long silence follows. I worry that the Zeta brothers require this acrobatic poses and tickles in order to get ready to practice their craft. I nibble on my thumbnail. It is something I do when concerned. These three seem rather unstable. *Perhaps there are other mages we can find?*

"Look," says Rhodes. "Kaps needs to be fixed up in time for tomorrow's birthday dinner and concert. Do your thing or I'll find someone who will."

"No need to be pushy," says Beta.

"It's my job," retorts Rhodes. He does not sound one bit sad about that fact, either.

With that settled, the three brothers launch into a long series of tests. I am poked. Asked to recite poetry. I let three drops of my blood fall on a handkerchief. They cast all sorts of colored poufs into the air and then discuss whether or not these little clouds react to me or not.

Overall, the Zetas hold many long discussions with fancy-sounding phrases like, *her refraction is idling the stereoscope.* I suspect they are out of ideas and making things up to pass the time. At one point, my Rhodes asks if they can cast a *parent search spell* on me, just to confirm they are able to cast correctly. This is a fine idea as I would like to know my family. However, the Zetas become extremely suspicious. My Rhodes quickly changes the subject.

A servant named Helga arrives with lunch. More tests follow. I give a snippet of my hair. Next I swoosh foul-tasting elixirs in my mouth before spitting them back out into glass containers. I even perform tests of balance and memory.

Helga returns with dinner. I suspect the Zetas are holding out for a day of free food, because once they've eaten, the mages inform us that they must take my test samples back to their laboratory. They will return in the morning with results.

This does not make me happy. My Rhodes seems just as displeased.

"You haven't tried one counter-spell," says my Rhodes.

"We fixed her hair and eyes," offers Alpha.

This time when my Rhodes speaks, there is a little growl in his voice. "That's not why I asked you here."

"We have other ideas for counter spells," says Alpha.

"So many ideas," adds Beta.

"We shall return in the morning," finishes Eta.

They slip out the door so quickly, you might think they feared my Rhodes would punch them.

It is not an unreasonable concern. My Rhodes already has his hands balled into fists.

Once the Zetas are gone, I focus on my Rhodes once more. "Thank you for bringing the Zetas here. I appreciate all that you do."

My Rhodes laces his fingers with mine. "We'll figure this out, Ves. These guys really are the best." He looks me over from head to toe. "You really do look like Kaps now."

"So?"

"How about we go outside for a little bit?" asks my Rhodes. "It's dark and I know a small garden that no one visits. And if anyone sees you, I won't worry that they'd peg you for *not being Kaps*."

At the mention of the word garden, my heart lightens. I've spent my whole life in a desert—at least the part that I remember.

Gracie has told me about green gardens. Excitement speeds my bloodstream.

"I would love this, my Rhodes! How do we get there?"

"Follow me." My Rhodes steps out onto the balcony and pauses. "Are you comfortable with climbing rock walls?"

I nod. "When the weather was bad, I would spelunk inside my cave."

My Rhodes grins, and I am pleased to see the small dimples in his cheeks. "In that case, you'll love this."

And in truth, I can not wait.

39

ZINNIA

O/*M* y Rhodes and I scale down the outer palace wall. Outside, there are many small stone buildings. My Rhodes says these are part of the kitchens. We slip past the small structures and into a line of trees beyond.

I had seen a forest before—back when we went camping—but this one is far more impressive. The trees tower above me, their broad purple leaves slowly swaying in the breeze. Great birds with pink feathers perch on the branches, cawing at us as we walk past. Fireflies light up the shadows with green clusters of brightness.

Soon my Rhodes and I reach a small clearing. Here, I find a fountain with the statue of a fire-breathing dragon in its center. Instead of fire though, water arcs from the dragon's mouth. Curved stone benches surround the circular fountain. It is small as a garden goes. I can see why few people would visit this spot.

All of which makes it even more lovely.

My Rhodes and I sit side-by-side on a bench. Minutes pass as we simply hold hands and watch the water cascade from the stone dragon's jaws. Overhead, the sky darkens. The cascade of red stars stands out even more brightly.

Pandora's starfall.

Sadness weighs on my soul. I still do not have my memory returned. There is no guarantee I shall be alive after Friday. This quiet moment with Rhodes may be all I have.

I wish to enjoy it to the fullest.

"Yes," says my Rhodes slowly. "There is something I want to tell you."

"Yes?"

"Well, not tell so much." He leans in closer. Our mouths are about to touch.

Happiness soars through my soul. I shall now kiss my Rhodes. If this is to be one of my final memories, then I am happy it is a good one.

Then the peaceful night shatters.

A small demon cat struts onto the grass. Releasing my Rhodes' hand, I crouch low to the ground. *Fighting stance.*

"What's wrong?" asks my Rhodes.

I nod toward my new enemy. "That creature is a demon," I explain. "I must fight it."

My Rhodes kneels beside me. "To you, that scents like a small blood lion, right?"

"Exactly." I partially shift so my hands elongate into claws. The feline nightmare stares straight at me, its yellow eyes filled with challenge. There is no doubt. I now face a small furry ball of evil.

"The thing is," explains my Rhodes. "Most pets here smell demonic."

I am intrigued, but not ready to lose my fighting stance. "Why is that?"

"They hang out with Furor. We're lust and wrath demons, after all. It rubs off. This particular creature is Lady Belle, the Cook's cat."

"Oh. So she is not a blood lion?"

"Nope, just a scavenger."

"Huh." I slowly rise to stand. "I did not consider that."

Now my Rhodes takes in a long breath. "I scent humans."

I inhale as well. "Not just any humans," I state. "My handlers." I step backward. "We must warn the others."

"Agreed," agrees my Rhodes. "I must go and report this to my uncle. Do you mind returning to the room?"

At the mention of Kaps' chamber, I picture myself cuddling in her comfortable bed. The need for sleep washes over me. It has been a long day of being poked and prodded. I yawn. "Yes, that would be lovely."

My Rhodes eyes me once again. I am starting to learn his looks. This one means he is weighing something. "Before our trip here, what was the longest you'd ever flown?"

"That time we went camping."

My Rhodes pales. "That was only twenty minutes! I took you on a seven hour flight. How are you even standing?"

"I am a tough dragon." *Which is true.*

My Rhodes grins and I enjoy his smile very much. "In that case, my tough dragon, let's get you some sleep."

My heart sinks, which leads me to a big conclusion. Although it is nice to sleep in a comfortable bed, it would have been even better to kiss my Rhodes.

Assuming that was what he planned do. How would I know? Overall, the situation is very confusing.

Perhaps I do need some sleep.

40

RHODES

Once Ves is settled in bed, I slip off to find my Uncle Atlas. He lives in a stone cottage not far from my childhood home. And yes, I feel guilty about seeing Atlas before I greet Sienna, but I just can't risk time with my mother. I may be able to fool the Zeta brothers about Ves, but Sienna will intuit the truth in three seconds, tops. Plus she's incredibly loyal to Tempest and Portia. Sienna sees any withholding information from imperial couple as dishonoring Titan's memory.

Needless to say, I often spend days slipping Kaps back into Furonium while avoiding my mother. I consider sneaking around to be part of my job, even if the thought does make we want to take a shower sometimes.

This is different, though. Tonight, I'm not sneaking around to cover up for a headstrong princess who won't listen to anyone but me.

This is for Ves. Her life is on the line.

For the record, I also hate Lady Belle. Ves was right; that cat is definitely evil. No doubt, she's licking her paws and feeling very satisfied that she broke up my almost-kiss with Ves.

My almost-kiss.

I could have cheered when the Zeta brothers left early. All day long, I'd been thinking about the dragon fountain. Ves and I may not have forever together. We deserve one romantic moment just for us.

And I will *still* make it happen.

I step through the forest to another clearing. Uncle Atlas lives in a small stone house surrounded by a high rock wall. I cross through the gate, rush up the short flight of wooden steps, and knock on the chipped red door.

"Hello?" I call.

Atlas responds right away. "Come in, Rhodes."

I push the door open to see Atlas standing at a round wooden table. Leather-bound books line the walls. Maps are laid out across the tabletop. My uncle braces his arms onto the table's surface. The pose reminds me of Titan. Even looking at maps, Atlas seems ready to burst into battle. That's how Father saw the world as well.

I close the door behind me and that's when I see it.

Atlas is not alone.

Portia and Tempest are with him. They're wearing their formal get-up as emperor and empress. This is an official visit.

Uh-oh.

I bow slightly at the waist. "Hello, your majesties."

"Your majesties?" echoes Tempest. "We're way beyond that, mate."

"Hi, Rhodes," adds Portia.

Now, I do sneak around for Kaps. But I have rules. I'll only withhold information from the emperor and empress if it keeps Kaps more secure. Believe me, I tried reporting the princess' every move to her parents. Kaps would then disappear for months. So it's a balancing act. The question is always: *what's the best way to fulfill my duties as guard?*

This case is different. Now I'm face-to-face with the imperial parents. If they ask me a direct question, then all bets are off. I will not lie.

"We know Kaps is with you," begins Portia. "She got into some trouble with one of her enchanted artifacts. The Zeta brothers are besides themselves with worry. They can't seem to fix it. We're sending Mistress Cerys over to the princess' chambers in the morning. She'll sort things out."

It's an effort to keep my demeanor calm. I can't believe they discovered the truth so quickly.

Tempest focuses on me. "What do you think of Cerys doing an examination?" He is asking that question, to be sure. But the emperor is *really* testing if I will deny Kaps is here. That won't happen.

"Summoning Mistress Cerys is a fine choice," I say. "She's the most powerful mage in Furonium."

Tempest nods. He's pleased I'm not lying about someone being here with me. "There's more," says the emperor. "There were also reports that Kaps looked and acted in a strange way around the Zeta brothers."

"Here's the situation—" I begin. I'm ready to explain about the memory spell that affects Kaps when Tempest interrupts me instead.

"Save your breath, mate." Tempest shakes his head. "We all know how tricky Kaps can be. She's sent in body doubles before."

"Body doubles?" I ask. "Not that I know of."

"You don't know many things," declares Atlas. "Kaps has used body doubles for years And you've been completely unaware. I know because it takes Kaps some time to recruit her stand-ins. My spy network always gets me word."

The wood floor of my uncle's cabin seems to shimmy beneath my feet. I manage to get out a single word. "When?"

Atlas starts ticking off instances on his fingers. "She did it last year at the ceremony of Pandora's starfall. Then again, six months past, at the diplomatic ball. And eight weeks ago she sent a double to perform at some concert in Ohio on Earth. Seems she hates boring events. The body doubles help. Afterward, we debrief the doubles, gain insights, and send them off. Kaps then must recruit new ones."

I open my mouth, ready to say this can't be true. But sadly, it *is* rather likely. I recall each of the instances Atlas listed. Every time, Kaps acted strangely and offered up a pocketful of excuses. Actually, it was the same excuse over and over. *Cramps.* Hell, in Ohio I went to three different drug stores to get her feminine crap.

Loser, thy name is Rhodes.

Words blurt from my mouth. "I can't believe this."

"You're a loyal friend," states Tempest. "But you're too close to Kaps and she's out of control. Remember what I said before? You need to contemplate a new life direction."

Atlas focuses on me. "We could use you on the Enforcer Squad. We can't have Huntress off all the time on secret missions by herself." After father died, Atlas took over as Enforcer of the Realm. He changed the program into a team that includes Huntress.

"Is that where Huntress is now? Off on a secret mission?" I couldn't help but notice the lack of concern about Huntress' whereabouts.

Portia and Tempest share a long look. "We know where Huntress is," says Tempest. "That's all you need to understand."

"Here is what's important," adds Portia. "What we must know is where *you* will be in the future."

I get the idea here. Portia wants me to picture a life outside of watching over Kaps. That isn't easy. Making sure Zin's sister is safe? That's the last thing I can do for my lost rhana.

I rub my temples, like I can force my mind to process all this news more quickly. "But what if the person with me *really is* Kaps?"

"Mistress Cerys will sort it out," says Portia. "Kaps attends far more events than she misses. We just want you to be ready. Whether it's tomorrow or a week from now, Kaps will make her last misstep. We can't lose another daughter. She must be secured."

A chill settles into my stomach. "And I need to move on."

"With all respect," says Atlas. "I am not as hopeful about this girl actually being Kaps." My uncle gestures across the tabletop. An array of small red stones are placed on the map. "See these markers? Each one signifies a human strike team that's positioned just outside the palace perimeter."

I step closer and scan the red stones on the table. There are hundreds of humans out there. "That's why I came here," I state. "I wanted to let you know I scented humans on the air."

"As mortals, these warriors do not pose a threat," says Atlas. "But someone let them into Furonium. That same traitor gave them detailed maps of our mountain. Whoever it is must be caught."

My eyes widen. "That's why you aren't doing anything. You're waiting for the ceremony tomorrow."

Tempest nods. "The traitor will reveal themselves."

"And you think it could be the person claiming to be Kaps." *I can't believe this.*

"That girl is definitely a Furor," says Atlas. "The Zeta boys were able to confirm that much."

The chill I felt before now turns downright arctic. *Could Ves really be a traitor?* My mouth seems to start moving on its own. "What do you need me to do?"

"Stay alert," says Atlas. "Keep reporting in." His eyes flare with demon power. "And trust no one."

"Yes, uncle."

"Now get some rest," adds Portia gently. "You'll need your strength. Tomorrow will be an eventful day."

I bow again. "Goodnight."

As I make my way back toward the palace, I sort through

everything I learned. Has Kaps been playing games with me all this time... could the princess really have been swapping out body doubles on me?

Sadly, the answer is a big *yes*.

It's exactly the kind of thing that Kaps would do. But what about Ves? Is she truly some kind of spy? Could all her talk about being possessed by Chimera actually be part of an evil plan?

Much as it kills me, that could also be correct.

All in all, my first loyalty is to the security of the imperial family. I owe Zin's memory nothing less. When it comes to Ves, I must be prepared for a single fact.

Anything is possible.

41

ZINNIA

I sit on the overly puffy bed in Kaps' extremely pink bedroom. One thought repeats on a constant loop.

Today is the day.

I know the schedule by heart. There will be an early birthday dinner. A pretty red dress is already set aside for me to wear. After that, the ceremony of Pandora's starfall will start at sundown. I shall sing a song or two before the emperor and empress give some speeches. Attending these events is not something I wish to do.

Yet there still is no sign of the *real* Kaps.

And also no visit from my Rhodes.

This morning, a servant stopped by and said everyone was busy with the ceremony. She asked that I wait here for the Zeta boys to return with information on my condition.

At the time, I believed that to be the perfect plan. I am still tired after all my adventures and can use some rest. It was only a week ago that I was living in my cave and being trained by Gracie. This is a lot to take in.

As much as I wanted to use this visit to get information on

Kaps and my Rhodes, I pretty much discovered all I needed to know when I found the princess' *closet of closets.*

Kaps is a frivolous girl. She is not someone that my Rhodes would find interesting in a romantic way.

Which brings me up to the present moment. Although it seemed like a good idea to stay in this chamber, now it is early afternoon. With each passing minute, anxiety frays more of my nerves. I scan the room once more. The walls and furniture are pink. The odd decorations are human vinyl records that have been framed. There are no books.

I can't keep sitting here and do nothing.

At last, a knock sounds on the door. I exhale. This must be the Zeta brothers. They've returned with information about my memory block. I rush across the room and pull the handle.

It is not the Zeta brothers who greet me. It is not even Helga, the nice servant who brings me red sandwiches. It is a towering woman in dark robes whose headdress is a cascade of black feathers. She pins me with a knowing gaze from her almond-shapes eyes.

"I am Mistress Cerys of the Hexenwing Tribe," she says. "I understand you've lost your memory."

"That is correct."

"May I come in?"

"Of course." I step back and allow her to enter. She sashays into the center of the chamber and pauses. Cerys is the kind of person who fills a space by just standing there. I close the door and wait.

Cerys crooks her finger at me. "Closer," she states. I take a few steps into the room. Cerys raises her hand. "Stop!"

I freeze in place. *This is very odd.* "Where are the Zeta brothers?"

"Crying into their coffee," says Cerys. "They are devastated they couldn't figure out what is wrong with you. That is why I have been asked to step in."

"Thank you."

"Do not say such things yet," states Cerys. "You've no idea what I'm about to do."

Awareness prickles across my skin. Cerys is right. I'm in a strange land with a super-powerful mage and no sign of the one person I trust. Cerys could do anything here. *Who would be the wiser?*

Cerys steps around me in a slow circle. She wears similar black leathers to the Zeta brothers, only her look is paired with a long cloak. She pauses before me.

"You are not who you seem," she says.

I debate about lying, but there has been enough of that already. "No, I am not."

"Do you wish answers about your past? It may not be what you want."

I look around the chamber, as if the response to Cerys will be written on the pink walls. Do I want answers even if it means my death? Or losing my family? There really is only one response.

"I am a warrior. Give me the truth."

The flicker of a smile rounds Cerys' mouth, but it is gone too quickly to be certain. "Your actual self is hidden," says Cerys. "Even I cannot see your true nature. I've never encountered anything like this before. The reality of your identity is a mystery, yet I have other skills rather than undoing memory spells." She widens her eyes. "I see glimpses of the future."

"And?"

"You will be asked to attend the dinner and ceremony. The truth will be given to you there. It shall result in your death."

Tears prickle my eyes. "What about my family? I do not remember them, but I know they exist. Will they be safe?"

Cerys closes her eyes for a long moment. When she opens them again, lines of sorrow mark her regal face. "I can not see that."

In a strange way, her sadness gives me hope. Cerys wouldn't

feel badly if she didn't have sympathy for my plight. That means she genuinely wants to help me.

"If you were me, what would you do?" I ask.

"I would not attend this ceremony. Life means hope." Cerys steps closer. "The question is this. What will *you* do?" She points to the door. "I can spirit you away if you like. Take you places where no one will discover your presence. Hide you from the world."

"You would do that for me?"

"I have seen this in a vision. In some realities, it is something that I have already done. Now answer my question. What do you wish to do, here and now? Attend the ceremony or go into hiding?"

Hiding.

The word moves through me in odd ways. A weight of dread settles onto my shoulders.

"No," I say at length. "I already know what hiding will get me. Four walls and no answers. I will go tonight."

"In that case, allow me to give you one piece of advice."

"Please."

"We Furor tend to see magic as the greatest power of all. We refuse the simplest humans machine because it works on its own, without spells. Yet that human imagination in itself is a power. Ingenuity. Trusting in your non-magical skills. If you wish to get beyond this spell you're under, then you must move beyond magic. Find a greater energy and hold onto it."

"And what's that?"

"Something you must discover for yourself." Cerys offers me a grim smile. "Not very good advice, was it?"

I shrug and stare at the floor. "I am no mage."

"But you are a warrior. Keep fighting."

With that, Cerys leaves.

And I know that I am about to die.

42

RHODES

Formal royal meals are always unpleasant. They last for hours in the palace's main feasting hall, which is a lot of golden everything: chairs, tables, walls, you name it. The only thing that isn't gold is the ceiling. That's a dark arch many stories above our heads which has been perfectly tuned for musical performances.

On the floor, a long table divides the space. Tonight, this surface is covered with every delicacy you can imagine. Beyond the dining table, nobles and diplomats from many tribes speak in small groups.

At these events, I always wear body armor and play the noble knight and guardian for Princess Kaps. For her part, Kaps always has some unpleasant surprise set up for the evening.

Like scheduling a last-minute concert for all of Furonium.

Or swapping herself with a body double.

Things like that.

Tonight, Kaps has outdone even herself and decided not to show at all. And Ves will soon attend in her place.

Not that anyone knows this fact, except for me.

With any luck, we'll just have a pleasant fake-family dinner and move on with our lives.

I have the whole thing planned out.

It's too tricky now that Atlas, Portia, and Tempest know that Ves may be a body double. There are guards everywhere. If Ves and I run off now, they'll tackle us both in a heartbeat. But once the meal is over, perhaps I can sneak off with Ves and get her somewhere safe. There are some caves by the Wineton seashore where she could hide.

That's a good plan, but it's one from my heart. Meanwhile, my head has very different ideas.

From a logical side, it's quite likely that Ves is actually a clever spy who's been playing me all this time. Ves may act the sweet and lost warrior but in truth, she may plot to use Pandora's box in order to murder the royal family. And if so, then she's most likely in league with Killian as well as the Triumvirate.

This could be a disaster.

And Ves could be evil.

That's not something I can ignore.

I scan the crowd again. It looks like a large gathering, but half of these supposed party goers are agents of my uncle's in disguise. No one from outside Furonium has been allowed in tonight. Atlas says we can't risk someone from another realm being injured or killed. And Atlas is right.

All in all, everyone is here except for the royal family. Once the herald announces them, then the formal birthday dinner can begin.

I scan the doorway once more. Ves should step through any second now.

The hair on the back of my neck stands on end. *Is someone looking at me?* On reflex, I glare up at the far-off ceiling. The darkness seems deeper than usual. The room normally holds a particular echo.

Strange.

In fact, I'm tempted to scale the side staircase to inspect the upper ceiling when, at last, the herald appears in the doorway. "Dragon shifters! Tonight we celebrate the birthday of our very own Princess Kappa Psi Phi Sigma!"

With that, something unexpected happens. The Kathikon march into the room and take places along the walls. Normally, these guards cover the hallways and perimeter. Having them in the dining chamber itself sets my nerves on edge.

What is my uncle planning?

The herald speaks again. "I now present their royal highnesses, the Emperor and Empress of Furonium!"

Tempest and Portia saunter into the room. The emperor is all smiles in his sharp tuxedo. The purple sash that marks him as emperor angles from Tempest's shoulder to his hip. Beside him, Portia wears a flowing blue gown. Something in her cherub-like smile reminds me of Zin. A weight of sorrow settles into my bones.

Shake it off, Rhodes.

The herald's voice sounds louder than ever before. "And it is my pleasure to present the birthday girl herself, Princess Kappa Psi Phi Sigma!"

Ves steps through the doorway and my breath catches. She looks stunning in a red gown. Although she could pass as a double for Kaps tonight, to my eyes, there's no mistaking the open and forthright look in Ves' eyes. That's all her.

My body seems to move on autopilot. I cross the space, take Ves' arm and lead her to the correct seat at the table. Once she's settled in, I take my spot standing behind her. Ves glances at me over her shoulder.

"Won't you sit down?" asks Ves.

"No, my role is to guard you."

She gives me a sly smile. "I'd rather have your company."

"You seem to be doing fine on your own." I didn't mean it on purpose, but there's no mistaking the edge to my voice. I can't help but keep thinking about what Atlas said. All this could be an act from Ves.

"I am glad to fool you," she says lightly.

My insides twist with rage and worry. *Is Ves admitting that she's been tricking me this whole time?*

The softest strands of music waft on the air. I lean forward. It's Ves. And she's humming *Our Song.*

When I next speak, I take care to speak close to her ear and in a low voice. "What are you doing?"

"Accessing my magic," she replies. "It helps me stay calm. I can only reach my powers through music."

Every nerve in my body goes on alert. Zin was like that. My rhana couldn't touch her magical energy without music. Is Ves some kind of super-spy? Has she been researching Zin? Only a handful of people knew that Zin used music to activate her powers.

"Often I sing words and I do not even remember them right afterwards," Ves adds. "Like that night on the bus when we were sleeping. The words vanish as soon as I sing them. But do not worry. I still recall all the lyrics for Cool Daze."

For some reason, I can't seem to move from my spot by Ves' ear. She must have gotten information about Zin. That's it. And I played *Our Song* that night by the desert. Ves has perfect memory. She's just humming it again.

Ves reaches back and sets her hand in mine. It's something she's done many times over the last few days. Then her humming turns into words.

Oh but those hours were so lovely
Then I was taken forever
Yes I would give my life gladly
Just to have him beside me once more
Forget all the darkness and war

The moment freezes in time. She's singing the refrain for *Our Song*. It's the part we never got words for. I haven't played it for anyone but Zin, and then only without lyrics.

And those words!

Memories flip through my mind. How Ves only knew things about Furonium that would be fit for a child... how she easily passes for her twin sister Kaps... the way Ves accesses her magic through music... and knowing the secret refrain for *Our Song*. All this time, she's been singing the secret refrain for *Our Song* and forgetting the lyrics right after.

And most of all, there's the effect I've felt since spending time with Ves. This pull to be with her. Protect her. Love her. It's the bond of a rhana.

All of a sudden, I know something down to my soul.

Ves is my long lost Zinnia.

War cries sound from the ceiling. Long ropes unfurl as fifty humans slide down from their hiding places to reach the dining room floor. All wear black body armor and helms. The image of a tail is painted on their legs.

Ves stands and gasps. "My handlers!"

They all turn to her and salute. "Greetings, oh Vessel of the Future."

Oh, no.

After this, things happen almost too quickly to track. I scoop Zin into my arms and race for an exit. There are imperial guards everywhere. Someone tears Zin from my arms while others hold me down. Even more restrain the human attackers.

Can't Atlas see this is a set-up? What could humans really do here—they don't have any weapons!

All they wish is to take my Zinnia away from me again.

I won't allow it.

ZINNIA

I sit on the floor of a dungeon cell. Darkness surrounds me. Cold bites into my limbs. The nearby stones feel wet with slime.

Was it only ten minutes ago I was seated at a royal table with my Rhodes behind me?

Yes, it was.

Then why did my handlers appear? They were dressed for war yet carried no weapons. Perhaps they only wished to be tossed into another part of the dungeons.

Or they wished for me to join them.

I rub my arms for warmth and wonder what will become of me.

Cerys said coming to this night would mean my death.

Maybe that will find me sooner than I thought.

RHODES

*I*t's all over in minutes. Guests are guided off to safety. Zin gets dragged away. Her handlers are killed—if they're lucky. More are marched off to interrogation huts.

I find my uncle back in his cottage, updating his maps. A handful of his enforcer team stand nearby. There are a lot of smiles and even a few mugs of beer. The group is celebrating and paying no attention to my presence. That could help. I take in a deep breath.

Do this for Zin.

"Well done, uncle."

Atlas looks up from his maps. "Yes, it was a clockwork mission. You did what you were supposed to do by trying to save the princess and all."

I force myself to stay calm. "It is my training. I acted on instinct."

"I hope you realize the truth now. That girl was a spy. A plant. She was sent here to allow those foolhardy humans into Furonium. They all have the mark." Atlas taps his shoulder. "Every last mortal."

I know the mark. It's a tattoo of a three-headed dragon and means eternal servitude to Chimera and the Triumvirate. Those are the bastards who stole away my Zin.

"I do realize the truth," I confirm. "Do you think there were others helping her?"

Atlas points at my face. "Now you're thinking like an Enforcer. Yes, I do believe that. We're interrogating the humans. If any of them did have Furor help here, we'll find them."

I step closer to my uncle. "I suspect Killian."

"Take a number," says Atlas. He returns his focus to the maps. "We've suspected Killian for years. Can't pin anything on him, though. Even tonight, he has a perfect alibi."

"Did you ever consider that Killian might be using magic to cover his trail?"

Atlas sniffs. "No one has magic that strong."

"Pandora's box might," I offer.

"And it regains all its juice tonight," says Atlas. "That's all a rumor, though. Hogwash." He keeps moving the same marker on the map, back and forth. "Now what was I talking about again?"

I've seen this kind of confusion before. A bewilderment spell. Titan taught me the classic signs.

"You were talking about Pandora's box," I offer.

Atlas looks up from his maps and blinks. "When did you get here, Rhodes?"

That is definitely a bewilderment spell. And my uncle is no easy mark. My guess is that Pandora's box is clouding his mind.

"I only just arrived," I say. "You wanted me to interrogate the body double. She trusts me. I might be able to gain real information from her."

Atlas stares at me for a long moment. At last, he speaks. "Quite right. You'll find the little traitor in the old dungeons. Lowest level."

"Thank you, uncle."

It takes everything in me to only walk out of the cottage. My instinct is to run, but that would be suspicious. Once outside, it's a different story. I half-shift into my dragon form. Scales cover my skin. My muscles thrum with magic and power.

I take off for the old dungeons at top speed.

45

ZINNIA

This afternoon, I thought waiting in a pink bedroom wasn't good for my sanity.

I was a fool.

Now that I'm in a dungeon, waiting is far worse. Faces appear to me in the darkness.

Killian.

Gracie.

My Rhodes.

Each seems close enough to touch (or in Killian's case, disembowel) but then vanishes before I can make contact.

I vowed to myself that I would not cry here. Still, my chest contracts with hidden sobs. Gracie told me what happens to warriors in prison. If I die tonight, then I hope it is quickly.

Voices sound outside my dungeon door. I can not make out any particular words, only a low murmur.

Thwack!

Well, that sound is unmistakable. Nothing quite compares to the unique tone of one warrior's fist striking another's skull. A jangle of keys follows.

I rise and shake out my arms. This is becoming familiar territory. Gracie trained me for situations like this one. When you're imprisoned, a new jailer can try to steal you away. They often do not expect resistance.

This could be my chance to escape.

The door swings open. Flickering torchlight outlines a familiar form.

My Rhodes.

"Zin," he whispers. Moments later, he wraps me in his arms. This is exceedingly pleasant. My Rhodes wears body armor, which gives his hug extra solidity. The sensation is so pleasing, I almost forget he did not call me by the right name.

"Zin?" I ask.

"I know who you are," says my Rhodes. "You're the Princess Zinnia."

I lift my brows. This night is one of never-ending surprises. "Me."

"Yes, you."

A new voice sounds in the prison. "Yes, her."

My heart sinks. I know that tone.

Killian is here. And he's brought other warriors with him.

The inside of the dungeon is too dark to see clearly. Still, there's no mistaking the sound of another thwack. This time, it is my Rhodes who falls over.

"No!" I cry.

Summoning my shifter power, I begin to change into my dragon form. And then? Killian will feel pain.

"Not so fast, sweet Zinnia," says Killian. Metal bites into my neck. I know this sensation; it is a needle. My body turns numb.

I manage to chose out two words. "Kill me?"

"Not yet. This will just knock you out for a while."

I fight to stay awake, but it is no use. As I lose all consciousness, I hear Killian call out to his warriors.

"Take the Vessel to the stage," he cries. "And bring along her sister. We end this now."

46

ZINNIA

When I awaken, I find myself sitting on a performance stage made of dusty wood. My hands and feet are bound with rope. Before me, the velvet curtain is drawn shut. The murmur of an audience sounds from beyond the stage. Outside of that, the place appears deserted, save for one person.

Kaps sits beside me.

The princess is bound as well. Even worse, Kaps' face is bruised. Dried blood marks one corner of her lip. Her jeans and T-shirt are ripped. My heart cracks with grief.

"Oh, no," I whisper.

Kaps sniffles. "Killian wanted me to go out and perform tonight." She kicks at the guitar by her feet. "That creep already cast a spell to prevent the audience from leaving. Once I was done singing, then you were supposed to come out and get possessed."

"And you refused."

Kaps chuckles. "What gave it away?"

"The bruises."

Kaps shakes her head. "I am so sorry. When Rhodes told me

you were in trouble, I didn't take it seriously. And all the time, Killian and the Triumvirate really planned to inject you with the spirit of Chimera."

"Do not fret. My plight was not an obvious circumstance."

"False." Kaps nods toward my tail. "I should have noticed the arrowhead end to your tail. You're really from the Firelord tribe. That's why Killian wants to use you tonight."

"Please. Do not blame yourself for his evil."

But Kaps, it seems, is on a roll. "And you know the worst part?" she asks. "You're really cool. I wish we could have spent more time together." She sniffles again. "Maybe perform a duet or something."

Music streams through my mind. I picture Kaps and I singing *Goodbye Sunshine*.

Goodbye sunshine
Farewell stars
Forsake the future
Forget the scars

Magic stirs within my soul. The red crystal ball appears in my mind. Inside its depths, I picture a little girl lying on a courtyard. An actual memory returns to me. For the first time, I know the identity of that child.

The girl was Kaps.

And I recall something else as well. I volunteered to go with Killian in order to save Kaps' life.

Despite the sadness of the moment, a spark of joy lights in my heart. This is what I'd been waiting so long for—some real answers about my past. All these years, I have been working to protect Kaps, although I could not remember knowing her. Even so, I cared so much for the princess, I sacrificed my life. Knowing that is enough.

Kaps sighs. "It should be *me* getting possessed tonight, not you. I've done nothing except be a terrible person."

"Listen carefully," I state. "Even if I could change places with you now, I would not. It gives me joy to know you are safe."

Kaps' eyes well with tears. "You are too good."

"No, I am my true self, with or without all my memories. That is what matters."

A fanfare of trumpets sound. The curtain rises. On instinct, Kaps and I scooch closer together. There is comfort in having her near.

Bright lights sear onto our faces. Killian steps out onto the stage. As always, he wears his gray suit and sash of office. The audience falls silent. A few Furor murmur questions.

Is this part of the show?

Why is Killian here?

"I'd like you all to try something," announces Killian. "Rise."

Rustling noises echo in from the audience as they try to leave their seats. More voices sound, only louder this time.

I can't get up.

We're magically trapped.

Somewhere, a baby starts to cry. My blood heats with rage. Kaps warned me about this, but it is one thing to know an evil plan ... and another to see it in action. Killian used the power of Pandora's box to trap everyone in place. He wants the Furor to be forced into witnessing his horrible scheme.

Tempest and Portia are out there somewhere.

So are Mistress Cerys and the Zeta brothers.

This is awful.

It is a small comfort, but at least I know my Rhodes is not nearby to see this. With any luck, he is still passed out at the dungeons. Or I hope he is passed out. I did not see the result of his wounds.

Back on stage, Killian pulls out a small crystal container from his suit jacket. Pressing on the edges, he expands it into an unmistakable shape.

Pandora's box.

Killian holds the container high. "You all have been given a great gift: the chance to watch as I use the power of Pandora's box to launch a new era for Furonium."

More murmurs sound from the audience. People still are not certain if this is a joke. After all, Kaps has done some strange things in her time.

Killian must hear their words, for he marches right over to Kaps. "Behold your princess. She is beaten and silent, as she should always have been."

The crowd grows restless. More voices sound.

Free the princess!

Death to Master Killian!

If the prospect of murder upsets Killian, he does not show it. Instead, the Master Dragon steps before me.

"And here is the gift I have waited years to present," announces Killian. "Before you sits Princess Zinnia." He gestures to me.

I am not impressed. Killian is a liar and manipulator. He chose me because I have Firelord blood, certainly. But I doubt this claim of my being lost royalty. Surely, this is nothing more than theatrics.

Killian opens Pandora's box. A flurry of tiny red dots zoom out from the container and settle on my eyes and hair. A moment later, I have white dreads and bright blue eyes once again.

"See?" asks Killian. "Princess Zinnia is a perfect match for her sister, save for her hair and eyes. And you all thought her dead. Meanwhile, I have been training her to become the Vessel of our Future! Using Pandora's box, I shall place the very soul of Chimera into Zinnia's body."

A woman in the audience screams, "No!" Somehow, I know the voice is Portia's.

I can not allow this to stand. The people must know that Killian tells lies. I take in a deep breath, ready to bellow out the truth.

I am a Firelord.

Princess Kaps was my friend.

I sacrificed my life for hers.

Yet I am not your lost princess.

Before I can speak a word, fresh dots of red light fly out from Pandora's box. The bits of brightness pool on the floor for a moment before rising up into the shape of a man. The figure is red and transparent, reminding me of a ghost who's been dipped in blood. The man himself is old and stooped, but with the unmistakable air of evil about him.

Chimera.

At last, I find my voice. "I am not Zinnia! And I shall not allow this spirit into me!"

Although my hands are tied with rope, new restraints appear on my wrists. Bright red manacles. *Magic*. My stomach sinks. This is the symbol of my enchanted vow to save Kaps.

There is no choice left.

I must accept this evil spirit within me.

I hobble up to stand. It is not easy with my ankles bound, but if possession is to be my fate, then I shall meet it as a warrior.

The red spirit of Chimera marches across the stage. He steps onto the exact same spot where I stand. For a moment, we are a living human and transparent ghost, all at once.

Then the red molecules that make up Chimera's body seep into my own flesh. Across the stage, Killian stomps on Pandora's box, destroying it.

I know what that means.

For me, there is no going back.

RHODES

My head hurts like someone punched my lights out. Mostly because a pack of Killian's goons actually walloped me unconscious.

I struggle toward the performance pavilion. When I awoke, the dungeons were deserted. Kaps is still supposed to do her concert tonight. My guess is that Killian won't be able to pass up an audience for what he's about to do to my Zinnia.

Gritting my teeth against the pain, I force myself to run faster. Soon the great arch of the pavilion's entrance looms above me. Beyond that, I find the familiar domed structure that houses a large stage and rows of plush seats. I pass under the archway and race into the performance hall itself.

What I see is beyond belief.

Every seat is filled. All the audience stare at the stage in horror. Zin is there, standing proud and tall. The image of Chimera's ghost overlaps with Zin's beloved form. She screams at the audience.

"I have returned," cries Zin. Her voice is a mixture of her own and Chimera's. "Beware, all you who have supported un-pure dragon shifters. Our power is our blood. All scrubs must be destroyed!"

Some in the audience weep. Others cower. A few smile. None of them leave their seats though, no matter how much they try. No doubt, this is another spell from Killian and Pandora's box.

Speaking of that magical container, there is no mistaking how it now lays broken on stage. Killian must have destroyed it. The container's magic can never be used to undo what's happening to my Zin.

What a nightmare.

If there is one bright spot in this dark moment, it's that I am free to move about. I see Kaps on stage, as well as her guitar.

An idea forms.

Perhaps I can save Zin.

Kaps has given performances here before, so I know my way around. I sneak backstage. A few servants stand about, but all of them are stuck in place, same as with the audience. Magically frozen. I march to stage left.

There's a long moment where I soak in everything around me. It's part of my training from Titan. *Never rush into a battle without scoping out your ground.* And although I won't wield a sword here, there is no mistake.

This is still a battle.

Bright lights sear onto the stage. Kaps watches her sister in horror. Killian stands beside Zin, grinning from ear to ear.

And Zin? She's the best and worst part of all. Her body keeps flipping between her own and Chimera's. The bad part is that with each passing second, Chimera lingers longer and Zin fades more.

But the good part? Zin still fights this possession. That's my rhana.

Steeling my shoulders, I march out on stage. A gasp sounds from the crowd.

Killian barrels toward me. "No!" he cries.

I move into fighting stance, angling my body to create a smaller target. Killian closes in. Every line in my body feels like it's part of a hammer. I swing and strike Killian's right cheek.

Whack!

I follow up with a barrage of punches. Rage fuels my muscles and narrows my focus. A voice breaks through my haze of anger.

"Rhodes! Zinnia!" That's Kaps screaming. And she's right to yell. I came here to save Zin, not pound Killian into oblivion. I lower my fists. Killian falls to the ground, unmoving.

Turning, I see Zin still stands on center stage. Or, I catch glimpses of her. Chimera is taking her over more by the second. Racing over to Kaps, I scoop up her guitar and begin to play.

> *Gray or green or brown or yellow*
> *Your look could change just like the rainbow*
> *I wouldn't care*
> *It's what we share*
> *You're mine*

This is probably the craziest thing I've ever done. And considering how I'm Kaps' *go to guy?* I've done a lot of insane stuff. The audience quiets as they strain to hear. While I play on, the red vision of Chimera seems to become stronger, not weaker. The old man eyes me and smiles.

Chimera thinks that he will win.

He is wrong.

I go into the next verse and call to my rhana with my soul. *Please, Zin. Hear the music. Access your magic.*

> *Hold my hand and play in sunlight*
> *The trees all flower with buds on branches*
> *We laugh and play*
> *We waste the days*
> *There's time*

For a moment, Zin overtakes Chimera. It's clearly her, in her red dress, standing firm. *Yes!* I keep playing.

Oh but those hours were so lovely
Then I was taken forever
Yes I would give my life gladly
Just to have him beside me once more
Forget all the darkness and war

Next, Zin's voice sounds as well. Magic surrounds her form and the stage. The tune echoes out to the crowd, loud and lovely.

Gray or green or brown or yellow
Your looks could change just like a rainbow
I never cared
It's what we shared
You're mine
Forever you're mine
Somehow we'll find time

I lower my guitar and address my love. "You are my rhana, Princess Xi Iota Nu Alpha. Keep fighting." My voice breaks as I add one last thought.

"You have to live."

ZINNIA

*M*y world was darkness and hatred, the inner landscape of my evil grandfather. Now, music soars through my soul. Rhodes is here. He plays *Our Song*.

Magic flows into me and through me. Memories reappear.

I have parents.

A name.

A rhana.

Rhodes has stopped playing, yet the music continues. It's the audience. Every Furor in the pavilion is singing *Our Song*.

> *Gray or green or brown or yellow*
> *Your look could change just like the rainbow*
> *I wouldn't care*
> *It's what we share*
> *You're mine*

Rhodes and I wrote this as the anthem of my parents... Of a hope that Furor can see beyond bloodlines and into the inherent beauty in all of us. More power and magic flows through me than ever before. It is the energy of my people combining with the strength of my love for my Rhodes.

The red manacles appear once more around my wrists. I press fresh power into them.

Crack!

The loops of red metal shatter and tumble to the floor of the stage.

Next the crystal ball levitates out of my chest. I remember now. I'd been in the crypt when Killian placed it inside me. The crowd keeps up its song. Fresh energy powers my soul.

Boom!

The crystal ball shatters as well.

Now one final task remains. I must destroy Chimera. I lean into my magic, asking it what I should do.

The reply appears in my heart.

I must make the prophecy of Mistress Cerys come to pass. It is now my time to die.

49

RHODES

I can not believe it. The crowd keeps singing *Our Song*. Zin already shattered the manacles that bound her to her vow. The crystal ball of her memories also appeared and was destroyed.

This may actually work.

My rhana has her freedom and memory back. I step closer to her. This should be a private moment, yet thousands of Furor watch our every move.

"Zin?" I ask.

She stands a few feet before me now. I wait for the image of Chimera to vanish from her. It does not. Instead, both of them fade in and out of solidity.

Chimera is still fighting, too.

"My Rhodes," she whispers. "I shall free the audience."

At Zin's command, thousands of tiny red bits fly away from Chimera's ghostly body. The gleaming dots settle over the audience. The effect is immediate; there's a stampede toward the exit arch.

I move closer. "Free yourself, Zin. Come back to me."

"There is only one way to release us all from Chimera," she says. "The magic has told me what to do. I love you, my Rhodes."

With that, Zin's tail arcs in front of her. For a moment, the arrowhead end hovers over her heart.

Then it stabs her through the chest.

My Zin falls over, lifeless.

ZINNIA

The magic would not lie to me. It said the only way to destroy Chimera was to kill us both. My tail did not wish to cut me, but it heeded my wishes.

Agony like I've never known spears through my chest.

It is done.

As I crumple onto my knees, I keep my gaze locked on my Rhodes. If this is the last sight I ever see, then let it be him.

The world around me turns red, same as the ghostly look of Chimera. I hear my Rhodes call my name. Mistress Cerys sounds as well. She says that I am strong and while Chimera is gone, I am not yet dead. My parents appear beside me, a pair of ghostly figures to my eyes. Together with Cerys, they chant over my body.

Magic.

Cool comfort moves through my rib cage. The incantations of my loved ones give me peace. A single fact becomes clear.

My death shall be a good one.

RHODES

*I*t does not seem real.

Chimera is gone.

Zinnia lays on stage, her lovely red dress covered in blood.

I shiver. My rhana looks so much like Titan did when he died.

Cerys, Portia, and Tempest all chant over Zinnia's body. Bits of white light surround her lifeless form. I kneel beside them all, reposition the guitar, and play *Our Song*.

Zinnia lays pale and unmoving, but if there is any power in our love and magic, then I must believe in one thing.

We can bring her back.

ZINNIA

*T*he red haze around me stays. I hear chanting from my parents and the music of my Rhodes.

Little by little, the crimson look of the world returns to normal.

Opening my eyes, I find myself laying in my old bed within the room I once shared with Huntress and Kaps. My parents stand beside me. Mum beams.

"How's my little flower?" asks Mum.

My reply is a happy reflex. "Growing bigger every day."

Kaps steps closer. "You shouldn't have done all this for me."

I give her the side eye. "Maybe I won't next time." We share a smile.

A figure materializes beside Kaps. It is Huntress. I can not believe how much my heart races to see her.

"Little sis," says Huntress on a sigh. "You're back."

"It is good to see you." I try to prop myself up on my elbows, but my chest still hurts too much. "Where is my Rhodes?"

My parents share a strange look. Seconds tick by before Da speaks. "Atlas is at the door. He is your new guard now."

"Rhodes is taking on new duties," adds Portia. "You need to focus on your rest."

I lean back into my pillow and smile. My parents may think they are protecting me by keeping me apart from my Rhodes. But that will not hold.

There is no separating a dragon from their rhana.

53

ZINNIA

ONE MONTH LATER

I toss and turn on my bed. A pile of books wait on the table beside me. All of them have been read. Twice.

How much would I love a new book? Very much indeed. But my parents worry that excess excitement will slow my healing. I counter that I am well healed and strong, but they are rather obstinate. Mum and Da even made Kaps and Huntress sleep in different rooms. They do not wish my recovery to be disturbed.

Ah, my parents.

Sometimes, I think they would dip me in amber if they could. Not that I fail to understand. They lost me. And then Kaps went a little crazy.

All right, a lot crazy.

Slipping out from under my covers, I step toward my balcony. Pandora's starfall shines less brightly in the night sky. Cool air wafts through the curtains. A chill seeps into my skin, so I pull the tie on my silk robe a little tighter.

One moment, the balcony only frames the sight of a darkened forest and flickering stars. A second later, he is there.

My Rhodes.

My rhana.

He says nothing, merely crosses the space to stand before me. Kaps and Huntress have kept me apprised of his whereabouts. My parents sent Rhodes off for training in order to join the Enforcers. They did not see the irony in the fact that Killian's preparations divided me and my Rhodes once before. Now new warrior training separates us again.

Yet I never doubted he would return to me.

Rhodes cups my face in his hands. The touch is both warm and electric. My body melts to be so near to him. Moonlight dances across his high cheekbones and strong jawline. His green eyes flicker with desire.

Still silent, he guides my mouth to his. At first, our kiss is gentle. A simple sweep of our lips. Then my Rhodes licks along the seam of my mouth, tempting me to open for him.

So I do.

Our kiss deepens. Suddenly, it's as if I can't close enough to my rhana. Our bodies press together, shifting in a dance that has a rhythm all its own. The electric charge of magic surrounds us.

My Rhodes breaks the kiss. "I've been wanting to do that since the night of the dragon fountain."

I run my palms along the planes of muscle on his back. "How long do I have you?"

"Not long. Visiting here requires a co-conspirator who is less than willing."

A gentle knock sounds at my bedroom door. It opens with a slow creak. "The imperials are coming," hisses a man's voice.

"Is that—?"

"Yes," replies my Rhodes. "It's Atlas—your guard and my accomplice." He pulls me more closely against him. "*Our Song* talks about finding time. It will happen for us, Zinnia."

"Move out, soldier," hisses Atlas.

My Rhodes gives me one last gentle kiss. "I'm sorry it has to be this way."

"I don't care," I counter. "How does the song go? You're mine."

"Yes," says my Rhodes. "Forever."

My Rhodes then steps off onto the balcony. For a moment, I watch his strong form outlined in the moonlight. Then my rhana is gone. I brush my fingertips across my lips and grin.

We will find time.

EPILOGUE

ZINNIA

MONTHS LATER

*K*aps, Huntress and I all sit about a small swimming pool. This is one of the newer additions to the tower complex. Mum and Da feel guilty about locking up Kaps, so they make constant improvements.

Yet my parents are a bit naive.

This is Kaps; she escapes often.

We three sisters sit in a row, wearing different colored sundresses. The pool is a pretty one: Furor-made and surrounded by palms. These trees are a special addition brought in from Earth.

As I said, Mum and Da feel guilty.

Kaps holds a data pad in her hands. "Have you seen this?" she asks while turning the screen in my direction. "You went viral."

I am still learning these odd phrases. "Viral?" I ask. "Am I sick?"

"No, you're famous." Kaps reads from the screen. *"Little did MusikGirl3000 suspect that when she uploaded a video of the band Cool Daze to WebTube, it would change the face of the music industry.*

Within twenty-four hours, the posting gained fifty million views. Fans have even started a petition to get the band to come out of hiding."

Huntress leans back on her hands and allows the sunlight to warm her face. "What is your scheme?"

I share a sly look with Huntress. *Of course, Kaps already has a plan here.*

"We reform Cool Daze," explains Kaps. "Get Rhodes out of military *whatever it is*. I'll be your manager. It's the only thing I was really good at anyway."

Huntress nods. "I think this is an excellent idea."

Kaps gasps. "You do?"

"Yes," states Huntress. "Killian is still at large."

I frown. "I do not follow."

My Rhodes almost beat Killian to death, but someone that evil never dies when you wish it. The old Master Dragon slipped off and hasn't been seen again.

"I have reports Killian is on Earth," declares Huntress. "He has new humans following him. If Cool Daze reforms, then that would act as an excellent decoy to drag Killian out of hiding. We can bring him to justice."

I smile at the thought. "That would be enjoyable." The longer I am free from my magical vow, the angrier I grow with the old Master Dragon.

"And there are other loose ends to tie off on Earth," adds Huntress. "Like Chase."

"You mean, Chase You Dick?" I ask.

"That's the one," says Huntress. "He is a rather shady character. We should lure him out of hiding as well."

Kaps kicks the water and grins. "This is the best! We're going on tour again."

"But what about Mum and Da?" I ask. "You have to get out of this tower, Kaps." It is true that Huntress and I can come and go, but Kaps must stay put. At least, that is the situation so far. Rumors are, all three of us may be forced to stay here.

Kaps rolls her eyes. "You know that's not a problem for me."

"Not a problem for an hour or two," I say. "But this is a tour we are talking about. That takes weeks of travel. And my Rhodes must come along as well. Yet Mum and Da have not accepted our status as rhanas."

Kaps waves her hand dismissively. "Leave it all to me. I'll work it out."

And in that moment, I know precisely what will happen.

Very soon, we shall all be off on tour.

∽

—The End—

The adventure continues with RHODES (Angelbound Offspring #4).
Read on for a sample!

ALSO BY CHRISTINA BAUER

RHODES

The adventure continues *with RHODES (Angelbound Offspring #4).*
Read on for a sample!

ANGELBOUND

Revisit ANGELBOUND, the kick-ass paranormal romance with more than 1 million copies sold!

LINCOLN

Enjoy Lincoln's perspective with the Angelbound LINCOLN series!

FAIRY TALES OF THE MAGICORUM

A modern fairy tale that *USA Today* calls a 'must-read!' Check out
WOLVES AND ROSES!

DIMENSION DRIFT

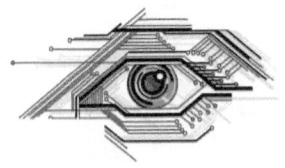

A kick-ass heroine + a swoon-worthy prince + an all-girl heist =
the DIMENSION DRIFT series!

BEHOLDER

Medieval mages ... Slow-burn love ... And heart-pounding action! Check out the BEHOLDER series!

PIXIELAND DIARIES

PIXIELAND DIARIES tells the story of sassy pixie Calla and 'her' elf prince, Dare.

CHAPTER ONE - ZINNIA'S VOICE

I may be a princess trapped in a tower, yet I am a happy one. Why? My Rhodes sits nearby, strumming a new rhythm on his acoustic guitar.

Ah, sweet music.

The tower itself is called the Dragon's Claw, for it resembles a huge talon that arcs up from ground. All around it, red desert stretches off in every direction.

Yes, it is a prison.

Happily I am on good terms with the warden, who is my sister, Huntress. My parents placed me and my sisters in this tower—that means Kaps is here as well—along with specific instructions for Huntress. Mum and Da trust her judgment. When Huntress tells the guards to look the other way, that's what happens. Tonight, Huntress ordered the tower's rooftop terrace to be vacated. Now I may enjoy *alone time* with my fated mate, what we dragon shifters call our *rhana*.

It is much appreciated.

Leaning back on my lawn chair, I stare up at the night sky. My Rhodes plays on. The new tune wraps about my soul. Staccato notes pluck at my heart. Long chords follow, moving into a slow refrain that captures Rhode's inner strength. The song ends. I sigh.

"That was lovely. "

"Thank you."

With the tune has ended, I refocus on Rhodes once more. He is tall and lean with whip-strong muscle. While I've been in the Dragon's Claw, my Rhodes has been training to join the Kathikon, the Emperor's Guard. The work has paid off. My rhana's shoulders, arms, and legs now bulge with muscle. His brown hair is cropped short; I long to run my fingers across the shorter cut. He fixes me with his moss-green eyes.

How long have I just been staring at him? Too long, possibly.

I clear my throat. "I've no lyrics for you yet."

"Not a worry. I know you'll come up with something lovely."

Usually, I must hear a new tune at least three times before lyrics appear. These first listens are the best, though. I am not torturing myself to find the right phrase or rhyme. The song simply moves through me.

"Please play it again and soon," I say.

"Happy to oblige."

My Rhodes grins, and his long lashes add extra emphasis to any expression. The sight makes my heart spark. Turning, he resets his guitar into its case. This is a careful business, by the way. My Rhodes worked hard to rebuild one of his old childhood instruments. Now, any scratch on that guitar would feel like a deep wound to both of us.

While my Rhodes finishes his work, I really soak in my surroundings once more. The roof terrace holds little. Huntress, Kaps and I dragged up a trio of lawn chairs. That's about it. My parents say we must live here for our safety, yet they give few specifics. And Mum and Da rarely visit, so we've had little chance to get more information. Still, Huntress believes it is serious, and I trust her.

That's when I notice something new.

"Is that a picnic basket?" I ask.

My Rhodes carefully closes his guitar case with a small click. "It is."

I spent years being held by the Triumvirate on Earth. During that time, my sole source of nutrition was dried protein bars. When I first escaped, I tried all sorts of foods. That didn't end well. Now I only eat plain burgers. My Rhodes has been worried. He wishes to expand my diet.

My Rhodes opens a basket. Small containers line the interior. "I brought things we can taste together."

On reflex, my mouth scrunches into a frown of disgust. "There is no forgetting the last thing I tried."

"Dried chili peppers are not meant to be eaten by the handful."

I count off more culinary disasters. "Or pickles. Or salt. Or cinnamon. The things eaten here are disgusting. I like my burgers."

My Rhodes shoots me a sly look. He knows that after that song, I'll do just about anything he asks. "How about this?" He opens a small container and takes out a little red thing.

"Is that bloody? I won't eat anything that drips blood."

"It's not bloody. It's a strawberry."

Vague memories sift through the back of my mind. I recall my life as a child, before I was taken by the Triumvirate. Sunshine spilled out over a bowl of red fruit topped with cream. *Strawberries. Delicious.* Sitting upright and sideways on my chair, I reach toward the fruit and stop myself.

Delicious, my foot. I also thought that about the dried chili peppers.

My Rhodes sits down beside me on the lawn chair. He holds up a strawberry and pops it in his mouth. "Mmmmm." Then, he offers another one to me.

I scooch away from him an inch. "Still looks bloody."

My Rhodes chuckles. I love the way the moonlight outlines

his strong frame as his shoulders shake with laughter. "I've an idea." My Rhodes reaches into the basket and pulls out a long checkered napkin. "Cover your eyes and you won't see a thing."

I am Furor. Our powers cover the mortal sins of lust and wrath. At this suggestion, something stirs inside me. All of a sudden, I can't think of anything I want more than to have my eyes covered while My Rhodes does anything. I'd even try more chili peppers if he asked.

"All right." My heart thuds faster against my rib cage.

With gentle movements, my Rhodes rolls the napkin into a band that he ties over my eyes. "Comfortable?"

I nod. To be honest, I'm perhaps a little intrigued here.

All right, far more than a *little* intrigued.

"Ready for your first taste?" asks my Rhodes. His voice is the perfect mixture of growly and sweet.

"Yes."

I open my mouth and my Rhodes sets a round something on my tongue. I try to speak past the shape, but it's not easy. "Isth bumpy."

"Those are tiny seeds. They don't taste like anything. You need to bite down to get the real flavor."

What kind of taste will I find?

I test the item out on my tongue. It certainly doesn't have the coppery tang of blood. Little by little, I bite down. The flavor bursts with the sweet taste of summer. I chew quickly and swallow. "I remember! Huntress, Kaps, and I ate these when we were little! Great bowls of strawberries and cream!"

"Ready for another one?"

"Oh, yes." I open my mouth. This time, my Rhodes sets something hard and flat on my tongue. I bite down right away. It is starchy and salty. "Not bad."

"That's a cracker. Ready for another?"

I merely open my lips in reply. My Rhodes pops a small square in my mouth. I bite down into the most glorious flavor ever. It is smooth and sweet, creamy and dark, all at once. I stop chewing so I may savor the taste. Without meaning to, a single sound escapes me. "Mmmm."

"That, my lovely Zinnia, is chocolate."

With my right hand, I lift my blindfold up a little so I may shoot my Rhodes a sly look. With my left hand, I crook him closer. The meaning is clear.

Let's share.

~

End of Sample

Order RHODES (Angelbound Offspring #4) Today!

APPENDIX

IF YOU ENJOYED THIS BOOK…

…Please consider leaving a review, even if it's just a line or two. Every bit truly helps, especially for those of us who don't *write by the numbers,* if you know what I mean.

Plus I have it on good authority that every time you review an indie author, somewhere an angel gets a mocha latte. For reals.

And angels need their caffeine, too.

ACKNOWLEDGMENTS

If you're reading my freaking acknowledgements, chances are, I should thank you for something. So, for the record: you are awesome, dear reader.

That said, huge and heartfelt thanks must go out to my husband and son for their rock-solid support. Being an author means a lot of early mornings, late nights, long weekends, and never-ending patience. You two are the best guys in the universe, period.

After that, I must thank the extensive network of reviewers, friends and colleagues who helped me build my writing chops in general. Gracias.

Finally, deep affection goes out to my late, much loved, and dearly missed Aunt Sandy and Uncle Henry. You saw the writer in me, always. Thank you, first and last.

ABOUT CHRISTINA BAUER

Christina Bauer thinks that fantasy books are like bacon: they just make life better. All of which is why she writes romance novels that feature demons, dragons, wizards, witches, elves, elementals, and a bunch of random stuff that she brainstorms while riding the Boston T. Oh, and she includes lots of humor and kick-ass chicks, too. Christina lives in Newton, MA with her husband, son, and semi-insane golden retriever, Ruby.

Stalk Christina on Social Media

Blog:
http://monsterhousebooks.com/blog/category/christina

Facebook:
https://www.facebook.com/authorBauer/

Instagram:
https://www.instagram.com/christina_cb_bauer/

Twitter:
@CB_Bauer

VLOG:
https://tinyurl.com/Vlogbauer

Web site:
www.bauersbooks.com

COMPLIMENTARY BOOK

Get a FREE novella when you sign up for Christina's newsletter:
https://tinyurl.com/bauersbooks

BEVERLY HILLS VAMPIRE

A NOVELLA BY
CHRISTINA BAUER

www.ingramcontent.com/pod-product-compliance
Lightning Source LLC
Chambersburg PA
CBHW022025240626

47154CB00007B/2265